Dark Waters o

© Copyright 2024 - All rights reserved.

All rights reserved. No part of this publication may be reproduced, distributed, or transmitted in any form or by any means, including photocopying, recording, or other electronic or mechanical methods, without the prior written permission of the publisher, except in the case of brief quotations embodied in critical reviews and certain other noncommercial uses permitted by copyright law.

Legal Notice:

This book is copyright-protected. It is only for personal use. You cannot amend, distribute, sell, use, quote, or paraphrase any part of the content within this book without the consent of the author or publisher.

This is a work of fiction. Names, characters, places, and incidents either are products of the author's imagination or are used fictitiously. Any resemblance to actual events, locations, or persons, living or dead, is entirely coincidental or used as a reference for the story.

Table of Contents

Introduction 1
Chapter 1 Homecoming 2
Chapter 2 Unsettling Memories 5
Chapter 3 Strange Shadows 9
Chapter 4 Secrets of the Past 14
Chapter 5 Local Legends 19
Chapter 6 The Watcher 29
Chapter 7 Unraveling 43
Chapter 8 The Trap 63
Chapter 9 The Pursuit 73
Chapter 10 The Escape 78
Chapter 11: The Divergence 93
Chapter 12 The Resolution 98
Chapter 13 The Revelation 103
Chapter 14 The Exposure 122
Epilogue The Aftermath 129

Introduction

In this gripping psychological thriller, Claire Hawthorne returns to her coastal hometown of Topsail Beach, North Carolina, following her mother's mysterious death. As she investigates, Claire uncovers a sinister conspiracy that has terrorized the town for decades.

Joined by her childhood friend Maggie, determined journalist Ethan, and Jim, a local with insider knowledge, Claire races to expose the truth. They discover shocking evidence of illegal medical experiments and unexplained disappearances, all linked to a powerful group led by the mysterious Dr. Victor Holcomb.

With enemies closing in, the team navigates treacherous marshlands and hidden bunkers, desperately trying to stay one step ahead. Their journey culminates in a heart-pounding chase to Wilmington, where they must get their explosive findings to the media before it's too late.

As the story breaks, sending shockwaves through the nation, Claire and her allies find themselves at the center of a scandal reaching far beyond Topsail's shores. With justice in sight, they stand united, ready to face whatever challenges lie ahead in their quest for truth and redemption.

Chapter 1
Homecoming

The air was thick with salt, and the roar of the ocean seemed louder than Claire Adams remembered. She pulled up to the old beach house on Topsail Island, its familiar white wooden siding now weathered and gray. The house seemed to sag under the weight of the years since she'd last seen it, almost like it had aged with her mother. Claire killed the engine and sat there for a moment, gripping the steering wheel until her knuckles turned white.

It felt strange to be back. She had spent the past decade trying to forget this place and everything it had represented. Yet here she was, standing on the doorstep of the past. The wind blew, sending a shiver down her spine. She looked up at the house, the creaking of its wooden frame almost like a whisper. She took a deep breath, grabbed her bags, and stepped out of the car.

Her first stop was the key hidden under the old seashell by the front door, her mother's idea of a clever hiding spot. Claire's fingers brushed against the cold metal of the key, and a wave of memories hit her, unbidden and unwanted. She forced them down and unlocked the door.

Inside, the house was eerily silent. Dust hung in the air like fog, and the place smelled of mildew and age. The furniture was covered in white sheets, ghostly outlines of what once had been. She dropped her bags on the floor and walked over to the living room window, drawing back the curtains to let the light in.

For a moment, she saw the beach as she remembered it, stretching endlessly into the distance, the sand glistening in the sun, the waves crashing in rhythmic certainty. But there was something off. She squinted, her eyes scanning the shoreline. Was that someone standing by the dunes, watching? She blinked, and the figure was gone.

Claire shook her head. "Get a grip," she muttered to herself. It was just the stress of being back, that's all.

She needed coffee, something to ground her. She remembered *The Daily Grind*, the local coffee shop in Surf City. Maggie, her childhood friend, still ran the place if Claire's information was correct. Maybe seeing a friendly face would help shake the unease that had settled in her bones.

Claire grabbed her car keys and headed back out. The streets were quiet, the kind of sleepy quiet that came with off-season beach towns. The locals were either hunkered down in their homes or at their businesses, preparing for the coming tourist season. She drove past familiar landmarks, the small, weather-beaten church, the surf shops, and the old pier. Nothing had changed, and yet everything felt different, like looking at a faded photograph of a place you once knew.

When she reached *The Daily Grind*, she parked and walked inside. The bell above the door chimed, and a wave of nostalgia washed over her. The interior was cozy, filled with shirts, mugs, and local art on the walls. The scent of fresh coffee and baked goods wafted through the air.

Maggie looked up from behind the counter, her face lighting up in recognition. "Claire? Is that you?"

Claire managed a smile. "Hey, Maggie. It's been a while."

Maggie came around the counter, pulling Claire into a tight hug. "Too long. I was so sorry to hear about your mom. How are you holding up?"

Claire shrugged, trying to mask the confusion and unease that she felt deep inside. "I'm... managing. Still trying to figure out what I'm doing back here."

Maggie nodded sympathetically. "It's got to be hard. Your mom was... well, she was a character, that's for sure."

Claire laughed softly, the sound foreign to her own ears. "That she was."

They chatted for a while, catching up on the years that had passed. Maggie filled her in on the small-town gossip about who had gotten married, divorced, and moved away. But as the conversation continued, Claire couldn't shake the feeling that Maggie was holding something back. Her friend's eyes kept darting to the window, and there was a tension in her voice that hadn't been there before.

"Is everything okay?" Claire asked, leaning in closer.

Maggie hesitated, glancing around as if checking to make sure they were alone. "It's just... your mom. Before she passed, she started acting strange. More than usual, I mean."

Claire's heart skipped a beat. "What do you mean?"

Maggie lowered her voice. "She kept talking about someone following her. Said she felt like she was being watched. I just thought it was... well, you know how she could be."

A cold shiver ran down Claire's spine. She had known her mother was unusual, even paranoid at times, but this sounded different. "Did she ever say who she thought it was?"

Maggie shook her head. "No, just said it was someone from the past. Someone she'd hoped she'd never see again."

Claire felt her mouth go dry. "And you believe her?"

Maggie shrugged. "I don't know. But I do know that after she died, people started talking. They say her death wasn't an accident."

The words hung in the air like a thick fog. Claire felt a knot form in her stomach. She had thought she'd come back to Topsail to put her past to rest, but it seemed her past was only just beginning to resurface.

Outside, the sky was darkening. Claire looked out the window again, half-expecting to see that figure from the beach. But there was nothing there, only the waves, endlessly crashing against the shore.

Chapter 2
Unsettling Memories

Claire drove back to the house, her mind swirling with what Maggie had told her. Her mother, convinced she was being watched? Was her death possibly not an accident? It was absurd, and yet Claire couldn't shake the feeling that something was wrong. As the sun dipped below the horizon, casting long shadows across the beach, Claire felt the familiar pull of fear creeping up her spine.

The house seemed darker when she returned, its looming shape cutting a sharp silhouette against the twilight sky. Claire stepped inside and flipped on the light, casting the living room in a dim, yellow glow. The old place felt colder, more alien than it had just hours before.

She crossed the room and headed for the kitchen, where a bottle of wine sat unopened on the counter. She needed something to calm her nerves, and wine would do just fine. She poured herself a glass, then wandered back into the living room, her gaze drawn to a stack of old boxes in the corner. They were filled with her mother's things, documents, photographs, and a dusty, leather-bound diary with her mother's initials embossed on the cover.

Curiosity stimulated, Claire sat down on the couch, took a sip of wine, and pulled the diary into her lap. She hesitated for a moment before opening it. The pages were yellowed and brittle; the ink faded with time. Her mother's handwriting was neat and precise, but there was an urgency to the way the words seemed to slant across the page.

October 12th, 2007: *I saw him again today. At the pier. I swear he was watching me, waiting for me to slip up, to let my guard down. I don't* *know how he found me after all these years, but he has. I feel it in my bones. It's only a matter of time...*

Claire's brow furrowed as she read. Who was her mother talking about? She turned the page, skimming through entry after entry, all of them filled with the same kind of paranoia. Mentions of a man following her, of seeing shadows in the windows at night, of finding small things in the house moved or missing.

She flipped further back in the diary, searching for a clue, until she came upon an entry from years earlier, before Claire had left for college.

March 3rd, 1998: *I've been so careful all these years, but maybe not careful enough. I saw him today at The Daily Grind. He looked older, but I'd recognize him anywhere. He was asking about Claire... asking too many questions. I need to protect her, but how? How can I protect her from something I did so long ago?*

Claire's hand trembled. Is someone asking about her? Her mother had never mentioned anything like this. Why would she hide it? And who was this man? She closed the diary and placed it carefully on the table, a growing sense of unease gnawing at her.

Needing air, she grabbed her jacket and stepped out onto the porch. Under the moonless sky, the ocean was a black expanse, the waves crashing relentlessly against the shore. She walked down to the edge of the dunes, scanning the beach for any sign of movement. But there was nothing, only the wind and the sea.

As she turned to head back to the house, a voice called out from behind her. "Claire?"

She jumped, spinning around to find a man standing just a few feet away. He was tall and broad-shouldered, with dark hair and a serious expression. For a second, her heart pounded, thinking of the shadowy figure her mother had written about. But then the man smiled, and recognition dawned.

"Lucas Harding," he introduced himself, extending a hand. "Detective with the Surf City Police Department."

Claire shook his hand, her pulse still racing. "Detective? What are you doing out here?"

Lucas glanced around, his smile fading. "I heard you were back in town. I wanted to talk to you about your mother's death."

Claire's heart skipped a beat. "You think something happened to her?"

Lucas hesitated, his gaze fixed on the dark waves behind her. "There've been some... irregularities," he said slowly. "A few things that don't quite add up. I was hoping you might be able to shed some light on it."

Claire frowned, recalling Maggie's words. "Maggie mentioned people were saying it wasn't an accident."

Lucas nodded. "It could be nothing, just talk. But there have been a few similar cases in the area over the past few years. Women going missing, strange circumstances. I'd like to ask you some questions, if you don't mind."

Claire crossed her arms, feeling a chill that had nothing to do with the sea breeze. "Questions about what?"

"Your mother," Lucas replied, his voice low. "And about anyone she might have been in contact with. Anyone unusual."

Claire considered this, remembering the diary. "She did mention feeling like she was being watched... she thought someone from her past had found her."

Lucas's expression darkened. "Did she say who?"

Claire shook her head. "No, just that she'd seen someone. A man, she said. But she didn't give a name."

Lucas sighed. "If you think of anything... anything at all, call me." He handed her a card with his number on it. "In the meantime, be careful. Topsail's a quiet town, but not everything is always as it seems."

Claire nodded, tucking the card into her pocket. "I'll keep that in mind."

Lucas turned to leave but paused, glancing back over his shoulder. "And Claire? If you see anything strange, don't wait. Call me right away."

Claire watched as he walked away, disappearing into the shadows. She felt a prickle of unease. What wasn't he telling her? Why was he so interested in her mother's death?

She turned and headed back to the house, her thoughts racing. Inside, she locked the door and leaned against it, her heart pounding in her chest. She couldn't shake the feeling that she was being watched. That someone, somewhere, was out there in the darkness, waiting for her to let her guard down.

Suddenly, a loud thud came from upstairs, startling her. Claire's heart leaped into her throat. She grabbed a flashlight from the kitchen drawer and slowly made her way up the stairs, each step creaking under her weight. The sound came again, louder like something heavy being dragged across the floor.

She reached the top of the stairs and pushed open the door to her mother's old bedroom. The room was empty, just as she'd left it, but the window was open, curtains fluttering in the breeze. She moved to close it but paused, spotting a small piece of paper fluttering on the windowsill.

Claire picked it up, unfolding it with trembling fingers. Written in large, messy handwriting were three words:

LEAVE WHILE YOU CAN.

Her breath caught in her throat, and she quickly scanned the room, her heart pounding. She shut the window and locked it, backing away slowly. Who had left the note, and how had they gotten in?

She didn't know, but one thing was certain: she was no longer alone in the house.

Chapter 3
Strange Shadows

Claire barely slept that night. Every creak of the old house, every gust of wind rattling the windows, set her nerves on edge. She lay awake in bed, staring at the ceiling, her mind replaying the day's events, the strange encounter with Lucas, the eerie warning in her mother's diary, and the chilling note left on her windowsill. Sleep finally took her just before dawn, but it was restless, filled with murky dreams of shadowy figures and distant screams.

When she awoke, the morning light was already spilling through the curtains. Claire sat up, feeling disoriented. She grabbed her phone to check the time, which was almost ten. She had overslept. Her mother's diary lay on the bedside table, a dark reminder of everything she'd read the night before. She reached for it but hesitated. The thought of reading more sent a chill down her spine.

Instead, Claire decided to go for a walk. She needed to clear her head, to shake off the lingering fear from last night. She put on a pair of jeans, a sweater, and a light jacket, then slipped the diary into her bag. Maybe she'd take it to the pier and read it there, surrounded by the bustle of people and the calming sound of the waves.

Claire stepped outside, breathing in the crisp, salty air. She made her way down the narrow road that led to the main part of town, past rows of colorful beach houses and small cottages. The sun was out, the sky a bright, cloudless blue. It was the kind of day she used to love as a kid—perfect for beachcombing or fishing off the pier. But today, the bright weather seemed at odds with the heaviness in her heart.

She decided to stop at the *Surf City Pier*. The pier was a hub of activity, even in the off-season. Fishermen lined the railings, their rods and reels poised over the water, while a few tourists wandered, snapping pictures of the ocean. Claire found a quiet spot near the end of the pier, away from the others. She pulled out her mother's diary and flipped it open to a random page.

May 22nd, 1998: *It's getting worse. He knows where I am, I'm sure of it. Today, at the beach, I saw him watching me again, his eyes cold as ice. How did he find me? I've covered my tracks so carefully. He must have someone helping him, someone who knows this place, who knows me. I have to be more careful...*

Claire shivered, even though the sun was warm on her skin. Who was this man her mother had been so afraid of? And why had she never mentioned him? She turned the page, her eyes scanning for more clues, when she felt a presence behind her.

"Excuse me," a voice said.

Claire jumped, her heart leaping into her throat. She turned to see an older man standing there, a fisherman judging by the tackle box at his feet and the worn baseball cap on his head.

"Sorry, didn't mean to startle you," he said, holding up his hands in a placating gesture. "I just saw you reading, and I thought I recognized you."

Claire blinked, trying to place his face. "I'm sorry, do we know each other?"

The man chuckled. "Not directly, no. But I knew your mother. Used to see her here on the pier, same as you are now. My name's Ray," he added, offering a hand.

Claire hesitated for a moment, then took his hand. His grip was firm, his skin rough from years of work. "Claire," she said.

Ray nodded. "I know. You've got your mother's eyes. She was a good woman, always had a smile for everyone, but she was... troubled, towards the end."

Claire's pulse quickened. "What do you mean?"

Ray glanced around as if checking to make sure no one was listening. "She started asking questions about things that happened a long time ago. Things best left buried if you ask me."

Claire felt a chill creep up her spine. "What kind of things?"

Ray leaned in closer, his voice dropping to a whisper. "She was asking about the old days, back when this town was different. Asked about the folks who lived here then, the ones who disappeared."

Claire frowned. "Disappeared?"

Ray nodded. "Not many people remember, but there were some... incidents. Folks just vanished with no explanation. The police never did much; things get swept under the rug in a town like this."

Claire felt a knot form in her stomach. "And you think my mother was... what, investigating these disappearances?"

Ray shrugged. "She approached me a few times and asked me what I knew. I didn't tell her much, but she had that look in her eye like she was onto something. Next thing I know, she's gone."

Claire's mouth went dry. "You don't think...?"

Ray gave her a hard look. "I don't think it was an accident if that's what you're asking. And if you're smart, you'll leave well enough alone. This town's got secrets, and they don't take kindly to folks digging them up."

Claire felt a cold sweat break out on her forehead. She wanted to ask more, to press him for details, but Ray suddenly looked over her shoulder and stiffened. "I gotta go," he muttered, grabbing his tackle box.

"Wait," Claire said, but Ray was already moving, slipping into the crowd on the pier. Claire watched him go, her heart pounding in her chest. What was he so afraid of? And who had he seen that made him bolt so quickly?

She turned back to the ocean, trying to process what she had just heard. Is her mother investigating old disappearances? And now she was gone, too. Claire felt a prickle of unease on the back of her neck, the distinct feeling of eyes on her. She turned slowly, scanning the pier, but saw nothing unusual.

Then, just as she was about to turn back, she saw a figure in the distance, standing at the very edge of the pier, half-hidden in shadow. He was tall, dressed in dark clothes, his face obscured by a hat pulled low over his eyes. He seemed to be watching her, unmoving.

Claire's breath caught in her throat. She blinked, and the figure turned, walking briskly away down the steps of the pier, disappearing into the crowd.

She wanted to follow, but her legs felt like lead. Who was that? And why did she have the unsettling feeling that she'd seen him before?

Claire decided she needed to get away from the pier. She quickly stuffed the diary back into her bag and made her way down the boardwalk. Her heart raced, adrenaline pumping through her veins. She passed a few tourists and locals, their faces a blur. She kept glancing over her shoulder, expecting to see the dark figure again, but he was gone.

She headed toward *Buddy's*, a small, local place just off the main road. The bar was a local hangout known for its cold beer and no-questions-asked policy. Claire pushed open the door and stepped inside. The dim lighting and the smell of stale beer wrapped around her like a blanket.

She took a seat at the bar and ordered a drink, her hands still shaking. As she waited, she overheard a group of men at a nearby table talking in hushed tones.

"Did you hear about the Adams woman?" one of them asked. "They say she was asking too many questions... just like the others."

Another man, older and grizzled, nodded. "Yeah, and now her daughter's back. Mark my words, trouble's coming."

Claire's heart pounded harder. They were talking about her. She turned to the bartender, a tall, dark-haired man with a rugged look, who was wiping down the counter.

"You're new," he said, eyeing her with mild interest.

Claire nodded. "Yeah, just visiting. I heard some... interesting things about this town."

The bartender's smile faded. "You're not from around here, are you?"

"No," she replied, "but my mother was. She was the woman who died recently... Helen Adams."

The bartender's expression darkened, and he leaned in closer. "Listen, lady, if you're smart, you'll do your business and leave. This town... it's got a way of chewing people up and spitting them out."

Claire swallowed hard, trying to steady her nerves. "Why do you say that?"

He shrugged, glancing around. "Because some things are better left in the dark, where they belong. And some folks... they don't like it when you go poking around."

Claire opened her mouth to ask more, but the bartender turned away, muttering something under his breath. She finished her drink, feeling more unsettled than ever.

As she left the bar, she looked around one last time, half-expecting to see the dark figure watching her. But there was nothing, just the quiet streets and the distant sound of the waves crashing against the shore.

Claire started back toward the house, a thousand thoughts racing through her mind. Someone knew something about her mother. Someone was watching her. And whoever they were, they didn't want her here.

But she wasn't going anywhere. Not yet. Not until she found out the truth.

Chapter 4
Secrets of the Past

Claire spent the next day combing through the house, searching for anything that might shed light on her mother's last days. The warning note left in her bedroom still haunted her thoughts, and her conversation with the bartender at *Buddy's* only added to her unease. Everyone seemed to know more than they were letting on, and Claire was determined to uncover what they were hiding.

She started in the attic, where her mother had stored a lifetime's worth of boxes. Dust pieces floated in the air as she climbed the creaky wooden ladder and switched on the single, dangling lightbulb. The attic was cluttered, a disorganized mess of old clothes, furniture, and cardboard boxes. Claire sneezed as she moved through the stacks, the scent of dust and mildew thick in the air.

One of the boxes, labeled **Helen's Things**, caught her eye. She pulled it down carefully, her fingers trembling with anticipation. The box was filled with old letters, faded photographs, and newspaper clippings. As Claire sifted through the items, she felt like she was piecing together a puzzle, a life she had never fully known.

She found a stack of photographs wrapped in a yellowing cloth. The first one was a picture of her mother in her twenties, smiling broadly, her eyes bright with youth. Beside her stood a man, tall and handsome, with a serious expression. Claire didn't recognize him. She flipped the photograph over; there was a date—*June 1982*—but no name.

Claire set the photograph aside and continued digging through the box. At the bottom, she found a collection of newspaper clippings, all from the late '80s and early '90s. Her eyes widened as she read the headlines:

"*LOCAL WOMAN MISSING: SEARCH CONTINUES FOR 23-YEAR-OLD KAREN MURPHY.*"

"*MYSTERIOUS DISAPPEARANCES HAUNT SURF CITY.*"

"*ANOTHER RESIDENT VANISHES—POLICE BAFFLED.*"

Claire felt a chill run down her spine. The articles all spoke of young women who had disappeared over several years, their cases never solved. The disappearances had happened in the neighboring towns of Topsail Beach and Surf City, all within a few miles of each other. She noticed that one of the missing women, Karen Murphy, had vanished in 1982—the same year as the photograph of her mother with the unidentified man.

Claire's hands began to tremble as she picked up a more recent clipping. It was dated just a few months ago:

"*UNSOLVED MYSTERIES OF THE CAROLINA COAST: A COLD CASE RENEWED.*"

The article mentioned renewed interest in the old cases, possibly because of her mother's death. Claire realized her mother had been collecting these clippings, probably in an attempt to connect the dots. She also realized that her mother had believed there was a link between the disappearances and the mysterious man from her past.

Claire carefully set the newspaper clippings aside and reached for her mother's diary again. She turned to the pages from the same year—1982—hoping for a clue.

July 5th, 1982: *He came to the house again today, asking about Karen. I told him I didn't know anything, but he didn't believe me. He knows something. I'm sure of it. I have to be careful... but I can't leave. Not yet.*

Claire's pulse quickened. Karen Murphy, one of the missing women, had known her mother. And this man... he had been looking for Karen, too. Claire wondered if her mother had known more than she had let on or if she had been afraid to reveal what she knew.

She decided to search the rest of the house, starting with the storage room. As a child, she had always hated it; it was dark and cold, with low ceilings and a damp smell that clung to the walls. She opened the door and descended the narrow staircase, the wooden steps creaking under her weight.

At the bottom, she flipped on the light. The storage room was cluttered with old furniture and boxes, much like the attic, but one area in the back caught her attention—a small door, partially hidden behind an old bookshelf. Claire moved the bookshelf aside, revealing the door. It was locked, but the lock was old and rusted. She searched around until she found a small hammer and chisel and used them to break the lock open.

The door creaked open, and Claire stepped inside. The room was tiny, more like a closet than an actual room. Inside, she found a single metal filing cabinet, dusty and covered in cobwebs. She opened the top drawer and began to sort through the files.

Most of the papers were old bills and receipts, but then she found something else—a manila folder marked **PRIVATE**. Claire opened it, her hands trembling. Inside were more photographs, this time of her mother, looking older and more tired. Some were candid shots taken from a distance, as if by a hidden camera. Claire's breath caught in her throat. Someone had been watching her mother.

There were also notes scribbled hastily on loose sheets of paper:
"She knows too much. Keep an eye on her."
"If she doesn't back off, we'll have to take care of it."

Claire felt a rush of fear. Her mother had been right. Someone had been watching her, threatening her. But who? And why?

She reached into the back of the drawer and found a small, leather-bound book. It was a ledger filled with names, dates, and locations. Many of the names were crossed out, some with notes next to them: *"Missing," "Unknown,"* and *"Deceased."* Claire's eyes scanned the pages until she found a familiar name: *Karen Murphy*. Next to Karen's name was a date: *June 1982*, and a note: *"Confirmed. Eyes on her friend, Helen."*

Claire's heart pounded in her chest. Her mother had been under surveillance for years, tied somehow to these disappearances. She needed more information, someone who could explain these notes. Maybe Lucas, the detective, could help. But she also didn't fully trust him. He had seemed too interested in her mother's death from the beginning. Was he hiding something, too?

She decided to start by visiting the *Blizzard Motel*, an abandoned place where her mother had worked years ago, as mentioned in the diary. The place had been shut down for years, and no one went there anymore. Claire grabbed her keys and headed out, determined to uncover whatever secrets the motel held.

As she drove, the motel loomed into view—an old, decaying building with broken windows and a faded sign hanging precariously by one chain. The parking lot was overgrown with weeds, and the building seemed to lean toward the ocean as if about to collapse into the waves.

Claire parked her car and approached cautiously. The door was locked, but she found a broken window at the side and climbed through it. Inside, the air was thick with dust and mold. The wallpaper was peeling, and the floor was littered with broken furniture and debris.

She moved carefully through the dark, empty hallways, her footsteps echoing. She headed towards the back, where she knew the office had been. As she approached, she heard a faint noise, like a door creaking open somewhere in the distance. She froze, listening, but she heard nothing else—just the sound of the ocean outside and the wind rattling the broken windows.

Claire found the office door and pushed it open. Inside, she found a desk covered in dust and papers scattered across the floor. She started searching through them, looking for anything that might connect the motel to the disappearances or her mother's past.

Then, in a corner of the room, she spotted a small door, slightly ajar. She walked over and pulled it open. The door led to a hidden room—a small, cramped space with no windows. Inside, there was a single chair and a table with an old tape recorder on it.

Claire's pulse quickened. She stepped inside and saw a stack of tapes next to the recorder. She picked one up and read the label: *"Helen—Interview 3."* Her mother had been here. She put the tape into the recorder and pressed play.

At first, there was only static. Then, a low and distorted voice crackled through the speaker.

"Why are you asking so many questions, Helen?" the voice demanded.

There was a pause, and then Claire heard her mother's voice, sounding strained and anxious. *"Because I know you're hiding something. I know what you did."*

The tape went silent, and then the voice spoke again, louder this time. *"You should have left well enough alone, Helen. Now it's too late."*

The tape cut off abruptly, leaving Claire in stunned silence. Her mother had been onto something, and whatever it was, it had cost her life. Claire reached for another tape when suddenly she heard a noise behind her, a soft shuffling sound, like footsteps on the old floorboards.

She turned around, her heart pounding, and saw a shadowy figure standing in the doorway, blocking her only way out.

Chapter 5
Local Legends

Claire's breath caught in her throat. The figure in the doorway was backlit by the dim light from the hallway, making it impossible to see their face. Panic flared in her chest, and she instinctively took a step back, bumping into the small table behind her. Her fingers brushed against the stack of tapes, sending them clattering to the floor. The shadow moved closer, and Claire could hear the soft, measured steps of heavy boots on the creaky floorboards.

"Who are you?" Claire demanded, trying to keep her voice steady. Her heart was racing, but she forced herself to stay calm.

The figure hesitated, then stepped forward into the light. It was a man, tall and broad-shouldered, with a weathered face and a grizzled beard. His eyes were dark, calculating. Claire didn't recognize him, but something about his expression sent a shiver down her spine.

"Get out of here," he said gruffly. His voice was low and threatening. "You have no business in this place."

Claire squared her shoulders, summoning whatever courage she could muster. "I'm looking for answers," she replied. "About my mother."

The man's expression tightened. "Your mother... Helen Adams?" He shook his head slowly. "You shouldn't be digging around in things you don't understand."

"What things?" Claire pressed, her fear slowly giving way to frustration. "What happened to my mother? Why was she here?"

The man took a step closer, his presence filling the small room. "You want answers?" he said, his voice barely a whisper. "You won't find them here. This place... it's cursed. Leave before you get yourself into something you can't get out of."

Claire opened her mouth to argue, but before she could speak, the man turned abruptly and disappeared back into the hallway. She hesitated for a moment, then hurried after him, but when she reached the door, he was gone, vanished into the shadows.

She paused, listening to the silence of the abandoned motel, then heard the faint sound of a door slamming shut somewhere in the distance. Whoever he was, he was gone now, leaving more questions than answers in his wake.

Claire felt a wave of frustration wash over her. She returned to the hidden room and gathered the fallen tapes. She picked one at random, tucked it into her pocket, and headed for the exit, deciding she needed to regroup. Maybe there were people in town who could tell her more, people who knew about her mother's past and whatever secrets this place held.

She left the motel and drove back toward town, stopping in front of *Quarter Moon Books*, a quaint little bookstore in Topsail Beach. Claire remembered the woman who owned it, *Nancy*, an elderly local who had been around as long as she could remember. If anyone knew the secrets of Topsail Beach, it would be her.

Claire entered the bookstore, the smell of aged paper and coffee greeting her. It was brightly lit, with shelves overflowing with books. Old maps, paintings, and curios lined the walls, giving the shop a slightly cluttered, almost magical feel.

Nancy looked up from behind the counter, her glasses perched precariously on her nose. Her face broke into a smile when she saw Claire. "Well, look who it is! Little Claire Adams," she said in a warm, raspy voice. "What brings you back to Topsail?"

Claire forced a smile. "Hello, Nancy. I came back to settle my mother's affairs. But I've found... I think she was involved in something, something dangerous. I'm trying to understand what happened to her."

Nancy's smile faded, and a shadow passed over her face. She put down the book she was holding and walked around the counter to where Claire stood. "Helen... yes, I heard about what happened. A terrible thing, losing her like that." She hesitated. "But your mother, she was always... different. She had her secrets."

"What do you mean?" Claire asked.

Nancy glanced around the store, then lowered her voice. "Come, let's sit." She led Claire to a small seating area at the back of the store, nestled among the shelves. "Your mother started asking questions a few months before she died. About old stories and local legends. She came to me and asked about the witch."

Claire's brow furrowed. "The witch?"

Nancy nodded. "There's a legend that goes back to the 1800s, to the days when Topsail was nothing more than a small fishing village. They say a woman named *Margaret Blackwell* lived here, a healer, some called her, but others..." Nancy paused, lowering her voice further. "Others called her a witch. They accused her of dark magic, blamed her for storms, shipwrecks, crops failing... and one day, they dragged her down to the beach and drowned her."

Claire felt a chill run down her spine. "And people believe this... witch is still around?"

Nancy smiled grimly. "Not in the flesh, no. But they say her spirit lingers, restless, vengeful. They say she cursed this place, that her descendants carry her curse. Folks around here have always been superstitious. Your mother seemed to think there was more to the story, though. She was convinced there was a connection between Margaret Blackwell and the missing women."

Claire's heart began to race. "Why would she think that?"

Nancy shook her head. "I don't know. She kept coming back, asking about the Blackwell family, asking if there were any left. I told her what I knew, but she seemed to think there was something... more. She was determined to find out. I warned her, told her to leave it alone, but Helen was never one to back down."

Claire swallowed hard. "Did my mother believe we were related to Margaret Blackwell?"

Nancy hesitated, then nodded slowly. "She didn't say it outright, but I think... I think she feared it. Your family's been here for generations, after all. Some of the old-timers in town still whisper about it. They say the curse never left."

Claire's mind was spinning. "And what do you think, Nancy?"

Nancy sighed deeply. "I don't know, dear. I don't put much stock in old tales, but I do know this town has a way of holding on to its ghosts. Your mother was a good woman, but she was caught up in something... something dark. And I fear she paid the price."

Claire leaned back in her chair, feeling overwhelmed. "Do you know if my mother found anything... anything concrete?"

Nancy shook her head. "Not that she told me. But she did mention the old Blackwell property, up near *Topsail Sound*. Said she'd been out there, poking around."

Claire perked up. "The Blackwell property? Where is that?"

Nancy gave her a cautious look. "It's up the coast, near the inlet. The house is long abandoned, falling apart now. No one goes there. They say it's cursed, like the rest of the family."

Claire felt a surge of determination. "I need to go there," she said firmly.

Nancy reached out and took her hand. "Be careful, Claire. Some things are best left alone. Your mother got too close, and look what happened to her."

Claire nodded, but her resolve was firm. "I have to find out the truth."

Nancy gave her a sad smile. "I know, child. Just... watch your back."

Claire left the bookstore with a renewed sense of purpose. She drove north toward the old Blackwell property. The air grew colder, the sky darker, as if the very world was warning her to turn back.

She finally reached a rusted gate, chained and padlocked, with a faded sign that read: *"No Trespassing—Private Property."* Claire parked her car, grabbed a flashlight from the glove compartment, and climbed over the gate. The path was overgrown, thick with weeds and brambles, but she pushed forward.

After a few minutes, she emerged into a clearing and saw the house. It was a large, two-story structure, its wooden frame rotting and covered in ivy. The windows were broken, and the roof partially collapsed. The air was thick with the smell of damp earth and decay.

Claire approached cautiously, the crunch of dead leaves underfoot the only sound. The front door hung loosely on its hinges. She pushed it open and stepped inside. The floor creaked beneath her weight. Dust and cobwebs covered everything. Broken furniture and shattered glass lay strewn across the floor.

She began to explore, moving from room to room, searching for any clue that might explain what her mother had found here. In a small study, she found a desk, its drawers pulled out and emptied. On the wall, she noticed a painting of a woman, her dark hair flowing down her back, her eyes piercing and intense.

Claire moved closer, her flashlight beam illuminating the woman's face. She looked strikingly familiar—hauntingly so. Claire's breath caught in her throat. Could this be Margaret Blackwell?

Suddenly, she heard a sound from upstairs—a faint, rhythmic tapping, like footsteps. Claire froze, her heart racing. Was someone else in the house?

She gripped her flashlight tightly and began climbing the staircase, each step groaning under her weight. As she reached the landing, the tapping grew louder and more deliberate. She followed the sound to a room at the end of the hall.

The door was closed, but the tapping continued on the other side. Claire's hand shook as she reached for the doorknob. The tapping sound was rhythmic, almost like a heartbeat, echoing through the hallway and vibrating through her fingertips. Claire hesitated, every instinct telling her to turn around and leave. But she had come too far to back down now. She twisted the knob and pushed the door open slowly.

Inside, the room was dark and musty, the air thick with the smell of mold and old wood. Dust swirled in the thin beam of light from her flashlight. The tapping noise stopped the moment the door creaked open, plunging the room into an unsettling silence. Claire's eyes scanned the space, her heart pounding in her chest.

The room appeared empty, except for a few pieces of broken furniture and an old rocking chair in the corner. The chair was gently swaying back and forth as if recently touched, but there was no sign of anyone else in the room. Claire swallowed hard, taking a cautious step forward.

Her flashlight caught a glint of something on the floor, a series of footprints in the thick layer of dust. They were small and delicate as if made by a woman. The prints led from the doorway to the center of the room, where they abruptly stopped. Claire's breath quickened. She followed the path of the prints with her light, moving it slowly along the floorboards until it landed on a single spot, a loose floorboard that looked slightly raised.

Claire knelt down, her fingers brushing against the excellent, gritty wood. She hesitated for a moment, then pried the board up with her fingers. It gave way with a reluctant creak, revealing a small, hidden compartment beneath. Inside was a leather-bound notebook, old and worn, with a faded cover that bore the initials *M.B.*

Margaret Blackwell.

Claire's hands trembled as she lifted the notebook out of its hiding place. She flipped it open, the pages crackling with age. The handwriting was neat but hurried, as if written in a state of distress. She began to read.

October 5th, 1862: *They come for me tonight. I can hear them outside, their voices full of hate and fear. I am no witch, but they do not believe me. I have seen too much, I know too much. They cannot let me live. But I will not leave this world without leaving behind my truth. My blood runs through this land, and my vengeance will be eternal.*

Claire felt a shiver run down her spine. She turned the page, her eyes scanning the hastily scribbled words.

October 6th, 1862: *I curse them all, every man, woman, and child who has sought my death. And I curse their descendants for generations to come. The ocean will be my witness, and its depths will swallow their secrets. They will know no peace, no rest until the truth is revealed.*

Claire's heart pounded as she read the final line, the ink smeared as if by a trembling hand:

My vengeance will not die with me.

Claire shut the notebook with a snap, a sense of dread washing over her. The stories Nancy had told her, the legends about Margaret Blackwell, were more than just folklore. Margaret had written about a curse, a curse that was supposed to haunt her enemies and their descendants. Was this why her mother had been so obsessed with the Blackwell family? Had she believed that their family was somehow connected to this curse?

Suddenly, Claire heard a low creaking sound from behind her, like the groan of old wood under pressure. She turned quickly, shining her flashlight toward the source of the noise. The rocking chair in the corner had stopped moving, but there was something else—a figure standing in the doorway.

"Who's there?" Claire called out, trying to keep her voice steady.

The figure stepped forward, and Claire's flashlight illuminated Detective Lucas Harding's familiar face. Claire's heart leaped in her chest, and a mix of relief and confusion filled her.

"Lucas?" she breathed, lowering the flashlight. "What are you doing here?"

Lucas looked tense, his eyes flickering around the room. "I could ask you the same thing, Claire," he replied, his voice low. "Why are you up here alone?"

Claire hesitated, unsure how much she could trust him. "I found something," she said carefully, holding up the notebook. "My mother... I think she believed there was a connection between our family and Margaret Blackwell."

Lucas's face darkened. "And you think this old diary is going to give you the answers?"

Claire nodded. "Maybe... I don't know. But something's not right, Lucas. My mother was afraid. She was being watched and threatened. And now I find this..." She gestured to the room around her. "What is going on in this town?"

Lucas sighed and stepped closer. "Claire, I told you to be careful. There are things here... things that have been buried for a long time. People don't like it when those things start to surface."

Claire took a step back, her distrust growing. "What do you know, Lucas? What aren't you telling me?"

Lucas hesitated, then lowered his voice. "I've been looking into your mother's death. There were... irregularities. And I think she was onto something, something big. But it's dangerous, Claire. Dangerous for anyone who starts asking questions."

"Who was she afraid of?" Claire pressed. "Who's been watching me?"

Lucas's jaw tightened. "I don't know for sure. But there are people in this town who have a lot to lose if the truth comes out. You need to be careful. You're walking on thin ice."

Claire felt a surge of frustration. "So what do I do, just leave? Pretend none of this is happening?"

Lucas shook his head. "No, but you need to watch your back. And if you find anything else, anything that doesn't make sense, come to me first. Don't go digging around on your own."

Claire nodded slowly, but inside, she felt torn. She wasn't sure who to trust—if she could trust anyone. "Okay," she said finally. "But I'm not leaving until I find out what happened to my mother."

Lucas gave her a long, hard look. "Just be careful, Claire. This town has its ghosts... and not all of them are dead."

With that, he turned and walked out, leaving Claire alone in the darkened room. His words echoed in her mind, and she felt a shiver run down her spine.

She glanced down at the notebook in her hands. If there was any truth to the legend of Margaret Blackwell, she was closer to finding it than anyone had been in over a century. But she had to be careful. If someone had killed her mother to keep these secrets buried, they wouldn't hesitate to come after her, too.

Claire took one last look around the room, then turned and headed back down the stairs. The house seemed darker and colder, as if it were alive, breathing with the secrets it held. She needed to get out of there, to get some fresh air, to think.

As she stepped outside, the wind picked up, whipping her hair around her face. She could feel the storm brewing in the air, a tension that seemed to vibrate through her very bones. She had uncovered something powerful, something dangerous. But she wasn't about to back down. Not now.

Claire glanced back at the old house, the shadows dancing across its weathered façade, and felt a chill. The truth was out there, hidden in the dark corners of Topsail Beach, and she was determined to find it, no matter the cost.

She turned and headed back to her car, her mind racing with possibilities, her heart pounding with fear and excitement. She had a new lead, a new direction. And she was going to follow it, wherever it might lead.

But as she drove away, she couldn't shake the feeling that someone was watching her, that eyes were tracking her every move from the darkness of the trees. She gripped the steering wheel tighter, her knuckles white, and pressed her foot down on the gas.

Whatever happened next, she would be ready.

Chapter 6
The Watcher

The sky was darkening by the time Claire pulled into the driveway of her mother's beach house. She had barely noticed the passing of the day as she navigated the winding roads back from the Blackwell property, her mind buzzing with everything she had discovered. The sense of unease had only grown since leaving the old house, like a shadow creeping over her, relentless and heavy.

She parked and sat in the car for a moment, staring at the house. The wind had picked up, making the branches of the nearby trees sway and creak. The waves crashed harder against the shore in the distance, the tide rising with the coming storm. Claire rubbed her arms, feeling a chill that had nothing to do with the temperature.

As she got out of the car, she glanced around, instinctively scanning the street and the surrounding woods. She couldn't shake the feeling of being watched, a prickling sensation on the back of her neck that had followed her since the Blackwell property. But the street was empty, the windows of the neighboring houses dark and quiet. Claire sighed and turned toward the house, her keys jangling in her hand.

Once inside, she locked the door behind her and leaned against it, taking a deep breath. The house felt different now, more oppressive as if it was keeping secrets from her. She moved to the living room, setting the notebook she had found on the coffee table. She stared at it for a moment, unsure whether she wanted to keep reading.

Her phone buzzed, breaking the silence. She picked it up and saw a text from an unknown number.

Are you alone?

Claire's heart skipped a beat. She quickly glanced around the room, her pulse racing. She typed back:
Who is this?
The reply came almost immediately.
Leave the house. Now.
Claire's breath caught in her throat. Her hands shook as she typed back:
Why? Who are you?
There was a long pause before the next message came through.
They're watching you. Get out.
Claire felt a surge of fear mixed with anger. She wanted to demand more answers, but before she could type another response, the phone vibrated in her hand again. It was a call, this time from the same unknown number. She hesitated, then answered.
"Hello?"
There was silence on the other end for a moment, then a low voice spoke, distorted as if through a voice modulator. "Leave, Claire. They're coming for you."
"Who? Who is this?" Claire demanded, her voice shaking.
But the line went dead, leaving only a dial tone. Claire stood there, her heart hammering in her chest. Was this some kind of prank, or was there someone watching her? She felt the familiar sense of dread creeping back over her, the walls of the house closing in around her.
She grabbed her jacket and the notebook, deciding it was better to leave for a while, to clear her head and think. She was halfway to the door when she heard it—a faint tapping sound coming from the window. Claire froze, her breath hitching. The sound was slow and deliberate, like someone tapping a finger against the glass.
She turned slowly, her eyes scanning the room until they landed on the front window. At first, she saw nothing, just the darkened street outside. But then, as her eyes adjusted to the dim light, she saw it—a shadow moving outside, a figure standing just beyond the glass.

Claire's blood ran cold. She moved closer, her heart pounding so loudly she could barely hear anything else. The figure didn't move, just stood there, watching her. She reached for the nearest light switch and flipped it off, plunging the room into darkness.

From the shadows, she peered out through the thin gap between the curtains. The figure was still there, cloaked in darkness, but now she could make out more details—a man, tall and broad-shouldered, wearing a dark coat and hat. His face was obscured by shadows, but his stance was tense and purposeful.

Claire's breath came in shallow gasps. She watched as the man slowly raised his hand, tapping it against the glass once more, his fingers splayed wide. The tapping was methodical, almost taunting. She felt a surge of adrenaline and fear.

"Who are you?" she whispered, her voice trembling, knowing he couldn't hear her.

Suddenly, the man moved. He turned away from the window and began to walk toward the side of the house, out of her line of sight. Claire's heart pounded harder. Was he trying to get in? Was there another way into the house that she hadn't locked?

She grabbed her phone again and quickly dialed Detective Lucas's number. It rang once, twice, three times before he answered.

"Claire?" Lucas's voice was tense. "What's wrong?"

"There's someone outside my house," she whispered frantically, her voice barely above a whisper. "He's watching me. I think he's trying to get in."

Lucas's tone shifted to one of urgency. "Lock all the doors and windows. Stay inside. I'm on my way."

Claire nodded, even though he couldn't see her. She quickly moved through the house, checking the locks on all the doors and windows, her hands shaking. She could feel her heart beating in her throat, her palms sweating. She glanced out another window but didn't see the figure anymore. Where had he gone?

She returned to the front of the house, peeking through the curtains again. The street outside was still and silent, the only light coming from a distant streetlamp. For a moment, she wondered if she had imagined it, if her fear was making her see things. But no, she knew what she had seen—someone had been out there, watching her.

Minutes ticked by like hours as she waited, every sound making her jump. The wind howled outside, and the branches of the trees scraped against the windows like fingernails. She clutched her phone, ready to call Lucas again, when suddenly there was a loud bang from the back of the house.

Claire spun around, her breath catching in her throat. The noise had come from the kitchen. She slowly edged toward the sound, her footsteps soft on the wooden floor. The banging came again, louder this time, followed by the sound of glass shattering.

Her pulse raced. She grabbed a heavy vase from a nearby table, holding it like a weapon, and moved toward the kitchen. The back door was partially open, the glass window shattered, shards littering the floor.

Claire's hands shook as she pushed the door open wider with the vase, peering into the darkened backyard. The wind whipped at her hair, and the rain had started, tapping lightly against the ground. But there was no one there. Just the dark, empty yard stretching out into the woods.

Suddenly, from the corner of her eye, she saw movement—a flash of shadow darting around the side of the house. Claire slammed the door shut, locking it quickly. She backed away, her breath coming in short, panicked bursts. She needed to get out of the house, to get somewhere safe.

She ran back to the living room, her eyes darting around for her keys. They were still on the coffee table. She grabbed them, but just as she did, the lights in the house flickered, then went out completely, plunging her into darkness.

Claire's panic spiked. She fumbled with her phone, turning on the flashlight. The beam cut through the darkness, but it also made her feel exposed and vulnerable. She turned it off again, opting to move quietly, listening for any sound, any hint of movement.

She reached the front door, her fingers trembling as she unlocked it. She swung it open and stepped out onto the porch, rain now coming down in sheets. She could barely see through the downpour, but she didn't care. She needed to get to her car.

She ran, her feet slipping on the wet steps, her breath ragged. She reached her car and yanked the door open, climbing in and locking the doors behind her. She fumbled with the keys, her hands shaking so badly she almost dropped them. Finally, she got the key into the ignition and turned it.

The car roared to life, headlights cutting through the rain. Claire's heart pounded as she put the car in reverse, her eyes scanning the rearview mirror. There was no one there, no sign of the man who had been watching her.

She drove away quickly, her tires skidding on the wet pavement, and sped down the empty street. She didn't know where she was going, only that she needed to get away, to put distance between her and the house, between her and whoever was watching her.

As she drove, her phone rang again, startling her. She glanced at the screen—Lucas.

"Claire," he said urgently as soon as she answered. "Where are you?"

"I'm driving," she replied, her voice shaking. "I had to get out. He broke into the house."

"Good," Lucas said, sounding relieved. "Keep driving. I'm almost there. Don't stop until you see me."

Claire nodded, even though he couldn't see her. "Who is he, Lucas?" she asked, her voice barely a whisper. "Why is he after me?"

There was a pause on the other end. "I don't know," Lucas finally said, his tone grim. "But whoever he is, he's dangerous. And he's not going to stop."

Claire's grip tightened on the steering wheel, her knuckles white. "What do we do?"

"We find out who he is," Lucas replied. "And why he wants you. But first, we make sure you're safe."

Claire nodded, her voice steadier now, "Okay, I'll keep going. Just... please hurry."

"I'm on my way," Lucas assured her. "Stay on the main road, and don't stop for anything."

Claire hung up and focused on the road ahead. The rain was coming down harder now, and the windshield wipers were struggling to keep up. She leaned forward, peering into the darkness, trying to stay calm. Her mind raced with possibilities, trying to piece together who could be behind this—who could be threatening her, stalking her, and why.

The headlights cut through the rain, revealing glimpses of the road, trees bending in the wind, and the occasional flash of a street sign. Claire's thoughts were interrupted when she noticed a car's headlights in her rearview mirror, approaching fast. Her stomach tightened with fear. Was it Lucas? Or someone else?

She picked up speed, her heart racing. The car behind her matched her pace, getting closer. Claire's grip on the steering wheel tightened as she glanced in the mirror again, trying to make out the vehicle through the sheets of rain. She could barely see anything, just the blinding headlights growing larger in her mirror.

She turned sharply onto another road, hoping to lose whoever was behind her. The tires skidded slightly on the wet asphalt, but she managed to keep control. The car behind her followed, staying close, its headlights flashing as if signaling her to stop.

Claire's fear spiked again. She couldn't stop, not now. She pressed down on the gas pedal, the car accelerating faster down the narrow road. The trees blurred past, the rain hammering against the roof like a thousand tiny drums. Her heart pounded in her chest, adrenaline coursing through her veins.

The other car closed in, its engine roaring louder, headlights flashing more insistently. Claire's mind raced with a thousand thoughts. Who was in that car? The figure from her house? Is someone else involved in this twisted game? She couldn't afford to find out.

Just ahead, Claire spotted the entrance to an old service road, partially obscured by overgrown bushes. Without thinking, she swerved hard, turning off the main road and onto the dirt path. The car bounced and jostled over the uneven terrain, her teeth rattling as she gripped the wheel. She looked back in the mirror and saw the other car zoom past the turn, its brake lights flashing as it tried to stop.

Claire didn't wait to see if it would come back for her. She pushed the car deeper down the service road, the path winding through thick woods. She slowed slightly, trying to stay in control on the narrow, slippery track. Her breathing was shallow, her heart racing as she listened for any sound of pursuit.

After several tense minutes, she reached a clearing. There was an old building, half-collapsed, with its roof caved in and windows shattered—a place she vaguely remembered from childhood, though she hadn't been there in years. It was a small maintenance shed, once used by the town for road repairs, but now long abandoned.

Claire turned off the car's engine, cutting the lights. She sat in the darkness, listening. All she could hear was the rain pounding against the roof and the wind howling through the trees. She waited, heart thudding in her chest, expecting the car to appear behind her, headlights blazing. But nothing happened.

She exhaled slowly, realizing she was holding her breath. Maybe she'd lost them—whoever they were. She knew she couldn't stay here forever, though. She needed to regroup and think about her next move. She reached for her phone to call Lucas, but before she could dial, a loud thud came from the back of her car.

Claire jumped, her heart leaping into her throat. She turned, peering into the darkness through the rear window, but saw nothing. Her hand tightened on the phone. She reached for the ignition, ready to start the car and drive away, when she heard it again—a faint, metallic scratching sound like someone was trying to open the trunk.

Her breath quickened. She looked around for anything she could use as a weapon and spotted the flashlight she'd taken from the house. She grabbed it, gripping it tightly in her hand. She opened the car door slowly, rain immediately soaking through her clothes. She got out, her legs shaking, and moved to the back of the car.

She pointed the flashlight at the trunk, the beam cutting through the rain. She saw nothing at first, but then, slowly, a hand appeared on the edge of the trunk, gripping it tightly. Claire gasped, stumbling back. The hand was followed by an arm, then a face—pale, gaunt, eyes wide with fear.

"Help... me," the figure whispered, their voice strained and desperate.

Claire hesitated, her fear momentarily replaced by confusion. It wasn't the man from the window—it was a woman, her hair plastered to her face by the rain, her clothes soaked and torn. Claire felt a rush of adrenaline as she stepped closer, shining the light on the woman's face.

"Who are you?" Claire asked, her voice barely audible over the rain.

The woman's eyes darted around, panic in her gaze. "Please, you have to help me," she said, her voice a choked whisper. "They... they took me. I escaped, but they'll come back. They always come back."

Claire felt her pulse quicken. "Who? Who took you?"

The woman shook her head frantically. "I don't know... I don't know their names. They wear masks, they keep everything dark. But they're after you, too. I heard them talking. They know who you are."

Claire's mind raced. "Why? Why are they after me?"

The woman's face contorted with fear. "Because of your mother... because of what she found. They think you know too much. You have to leave... you have to go."

Claire felt a chill run down her spine. "Where can I go? Who are they?"

The woman started to speak, but then her eyes widened with terror. She looked past Claire, into the darkness behind her. "No... no, they found us," she whispered, her voice breaking.

Claire spun around, her flashlight beam sweeping across the clearing. She saw nothing at first, just rain and shadows, but then she heard it—a low growl of an engine, headlights flickering through the trees. The other car was back.

Panic surged through her veins. She turned to the woman, who was trying to climb out of the trunk. "Come on!" Claire urged, reaching for her. "We have to go, now!"

But the woman was weak, barely able to stand. Claire helped her up, supporting her weight as they stumbled toward the driver's side of the car. The headlights grew brighter, the sound of the engine louder, roaring through the trees like a predator closing in on its prey.

Claire fumbled with the door, yanking it open and pushing the woman inside. She scrambled into the driver's seat, turning the key in the ignition. The car sputtered for a moment, and Claire's heart dropped. "Come on," she muttered, turning the key again.

The engine roared to life, and she slammed her foot on the gas pedal, the car lurching forward just as the other vehicle burst into the clearing. Its headlights blinded her momentarily, but she didn't stop, her tires skidding on the muddy ground as she sped away.

The other car gave chase, its engine roaring louder, closing the distance between them. Claire's heart pounded in her chest, her breath coming in sharp, shallow gasps. She glanced at the woman beside her, who was trembling, her eyes wide with fear.

"Who are they?" Claire shouted over the roar of the engine and the rain.

The woman shook her head, tears streaming down her face. "They're the ones who took your mother. They're part of it... the curse, the secrets... everything."

Claire's mind raced. "Why me? Why now?"

"Because you're getting too close," the woman replied, her voice breaking. "Your mother... she found something. Something they didn't want anyone to know. And they think you know it, too."

Claire swerved onto another road, the car skidding dangerously close to the edge. She fought to keep control, her heart hammering in her chest. "What did she find?" Claire demanded, desperate for answers.

The woman's eyes filled with terror. "The truth," she whispered. "And it's buried deep, deeper than you can imagine. And now they'll do anything to keep it hidden... even if it means—"

Before she could finish, the other car rammed into them from behind, the impact jolting Claire and the woman forward. Claire gripped the steering wheel tightly, fighting to keep the car on the road. She could hear the woman's cries, her fear rising to a fever pitch.

"Hold on!" Claire shouted, swerving hard to avoid another collision. She spotted a narrow dirt road up ahead, partially hidden by overgrown branches. Without thinking, she turned sharply, the car barreling down the path, away from the main road.

The other car hesitated for a moment, then followed, its headlights swinging wildly as it took the turn. Claire pressed down harder on the gas, the car bouncing over rocks and potholes, her hands gripping the wheel with white-knuckled determination.

She had to lose them. She had to find a way out.

The rain was a downpour now, blinding her view, but she didn't slow down. The road twisted and turned, a maze through the thick woods, but she kept going, her instincts guiding her. She glanced in the mirror—the other car was still behind her, closing the gap with every second. Claire's pulse raced, her thoughts a jumbled mix of fear and determination. She needed to think fast; she needed a plan.

The narrow dirt road ahead was slick with mud, the rain turning it into a slippery path. She pushed the car harder, the tires skidding dangerously close to the edge where the road dropped off into a steep ravine. Claire kept her focus, trying to keep the car steady, while the woman beside her clutched the door handle, her eyes wide with terror.

Then, up ahead, Claire saw a small bridge—a rickety old structure that looked like it hadn't been used in years. It was narrow, barely wide enough for one car, and the wooden planks looked rotten, but it was her only option. She glanced in the rearview mirror again; the other car was gaining, its headlights cutting through the darkness like a knife.

"Hold on!" Claire shouted as she steered toward the bridge.

The car hit the bridge hard, the wooden planks creaking and groaning under the weight. The tires slipped on the wet wood, and for a moment, Claire thought they might go over the edge. But she held tight, the car lurching forward as the bridge swayed beneath them.

The other car reached the bridge just as Claire's wheels hit the far side. She didn't slow down, racing toward the end of the bridge, praying it would hold. The other car hesitated, its driver realizing the risk, but then it too sped forward, trying to catch up.

Halfway across, the old bridge gave a loud, sickening crack. The wood splintered, and one of the support beams snapped, sending the bridge lurching downward. Claire's car hit solid ground just in time, but the other vehicle wasn't so lucky.

There was a deafening crash as the bridge gave way entirely, the other car plummeting into the water below. Claire heard the sound of metal crunching, the roar of the engine dying out as the vehicle disappeared into the water.

She didn't stop to look back. She kept driving, her breath coming in rapid bursts, her heart pounding in her chest. The woman beside her was crying, tears mixing with the rain on her face. Claire glanced at her, unsure of what to say, unsure of what to do next.

"Are you okay?" Claire asked, her voice shaky.

The woman nodded, still trembling. "Thank you," she whispered. "I... I didn't think I'd make it."

Claire tightened her grip on the wheel. "We're not safe yet. Who are these people? What do they want with me?"

The woman took a deep breath, trying to calm herself. "They're part of a group... a group that's been in this town for a long time. They're... they're protectors of the old secrets, the ones no one is supposed to know. Your mother... she found something she shouldn't have. They think you have it now."

Claire's mind raced. "What did my mother find? What do they think I have?"

The woman shook her head, her voice urgent. "I don't know exactly, but I heard them talking. They mentioned a name... Margaret Blackwell. They think your mother discovered something about her that could ruin them all."

Claire's heart skipped a beat. Margaret Blackwell—the witch, the legend that had haunted this town for over a century. "What does Margaret Blackwell have to do with any of this?"

The woman looked at her, eyes wide with fear. "Everything. The curse, the missing women... it all started with her. And your mother... she found the truth. The real truth, not the stories people tell. And now they think you know it, too."

Claire's breath caught in her throat. "And you... how do you fit into all this?"

The woman hesitated. "I... I was one of them once. I thought they were just a group of old-timers, protecting the town's history. But when I found out what they were really doing... what they were hiding... they turned on me. They've been keeping me prisoner ever since."

Claire stared at her, trying to piece everything together. "You said they took my mother?"

The woman nodded. "They did. I heard them talking about it. They were afraid she'd tell someone, afraid she'd ruin everything. They tried to scare her off, but she didn't stop. And then..."

Claire felt a cold knot form in her stomach. "Then what?"

The woman looked away, tears in her eyes. "They made it look like an accident. They... they said they'd do the same to you if you didn't leave town."

Claire's blood ran cold. Her mother's death wasn't an accident after all. "Do you know who 'they' are? Who leads them?"

The woman shook her head. "No one knows. They wear masks, they use false names. But they have connections—deep ones. They're in the police, the council... everywhere. They've been here for generations."

Claire's mind spun with possibilities. If this group was so powerful, who could she trust? She had to be careful, to figure out her next steps. "I need to find out what my mother knew," Claire said firmly. "And I need to end this."

The woman's eyes widened with fear. "No, you don't understand. They won't let you. They'll come for you... they won't stop."

Claire nodded. "Let them come. I'm not going anywhere until I find out what happened to my mother."

The woman looked terrified but didn't argue. "Okay... but you can't stay here. They'll find you. They always do."

Claire considered her options. "There's a place I can go, somewhere they won't look for me." She thought of Maggie and the small, cluttered apartment above *The Daily Grind*. It wasn't much, but it was safe—and hidden.

She turned the car around, heading back toward town. The rain was still pouring down, but the intensity had lessened. Her headlights cut through the gloom as she made her way back to Surf City, her mind racing with everything she had learned.

When she finally reached *The Daily Grind*, she parked the car in the back lot, away from the streetlights, and helped the woman out. She was weak and shivering, but Claire supported her, guiding her toward the back entrance of the coffee shop.

They slipped inside, the familiar smell of freshly ground coffee and baked goods greeting them. Claire's heart steadied a little. At least here, she felt a sense of familiarity, a momentary reprieve from the terror that had been chasing her.

"Maggie?" Claire called softly, moving toward the stairs.

Maggie appeared at the top of the staircase, her face pale with concern. "Claire? What's going on? You look like you've seen a ghost."

"I think I have," Claire replied, helping the woman up the stairs. "We need your help. We need a place to stay, just for a little while."

Maggie's eyes flicked between Claire and the woman, understanding dawning in her expression. "Of course, come up. You can stay here. But Claire... what happened?"

Claire shook her head. "It's a long story. But something is going on in this town, something dangerous. And I think my mother was right in the middle of it."

Maggie nodded slowly. "I always knew she was looking into something, but I didn't realize it was this serious."

Claire's eyes met Maggie's. "It's serious, all right. And I need to find out what it is before it's too late."

Maggie led them into the small apartment and locked the door behind them. Claire felt a momentary sense of safety, but she knew it wouldn't last. The truth was still out there, hidden in the shadows of this town, and she was running out of time to find it.

But she wasn't alone. And that was something.

Chapter 7
Unraveling

The room above *The Daily Grind* was small and cluttered, filled with mismatched furniture and stacks of books and magazines. The faint smell of cinnamon and coffee lingered in the air, but tension hung even thicker. Maggie had set out blankets and a pot of tea on the small kitchen table, but her eyes were filled with concern as she watched Claire and the woman settle in.

Claire's hands were still shaking as she poured a cup of tea for the woman, who had finally stopped trembling, though her face remained pale and haunted. Maggie sat down across from them, her expression serious.

"Start from the beginning," Maggie said quietly. "What's going on, Claire?"

Claire took a deep breath and recounted everything that had happened—finding the hidden notebook at the Blackwell property, the figure watching her from outside her house, the terrifying chase with the car, and finally, the appearance of the woman in her trunk.

Maggie listened intently, her face growing more worried with every word. When Claire finished, there was a long silence.

"So, you're telling me there's some secret group in this town that's been watching your family for years?" Maggie asked, her voice tinged with disbelief. "And they think you have something they want?"

Claire nodded. "That's what it looks like. And they killed my mother to keep her quiet."

The woman spoke up, her voice still shaky but gaining strength. "They did. I heard them talking about it. Your mother was asking too many questions. She got too close."

Maggie frowned. "Too close to what? A curse? Some old legend?"

Claire shook her head. "I don't think it's just a curse. I think it's something more... something real. My mother found out something, and whatever it was, it scared them. Enough to kill her."

Maggie looked at the woman. "And you... you were with them?"

The woman nodded slowly. "Not by choice. I didn't know what they were at first. They seemed like just a group of people interested in the town's history. I was new here, looking for work, and they... they brought me in. But then I found out what they were really doing."

Claire leaned forward. "And what was that?"

The woman swallowed hard. "They were... experimenting. Testing things. Looking for something, some... proof. They kept talking about the 'legacy' of Margaret Blackwell, about how they needed to protect it, to keep it hidden from the outside world."

Maggie's brow furrowed. "Protect it? From what?"

The woman shuddered. "From the truth. They think the truth will destroy everything. They've been covering it up for generations, doing whatever it takes to keep it buried."

Claire felt a chill run down her spine. "And what's the truth?"

The woman shook her head. "I don't know. I only heard bits and pieces. But they're convinced that if anyone finds out... if anyone connects the dots, it'll ruin them."

Claire turned to Maggie. "Do you remember anything about Margaret Blackwell? Anything that might help us figure out what my mother found?"

Maggie bit her lip, thinking. "I've heard the same stories as everyone else. That she was a healer, a midwife, and that some folks accused her of witchcraft when things went wrong. But... I don't know anything more than that. The town keeps the old legends alive, but the details are fuzzy, mixed with superstition."

The woman spoke again, her voice more urgent now. "It's not just superstition. I heard them say that Margaret Blackwell wasn't just some random woman. She was... important. She knew things, things that people wanted to keep hidden."

Claire leaned back, her mind racing. "Maybe she discovered something, something dangerous or valuable. And whatever it was, it's been passed down, hidden, protected by this group."

Maggie nodded slowly. "It's possible. And if that's true, it could explain why they're so desperate to stop you."

The room fell silent for a moment as the three women considered the implications. Claire's mind flashed back to the notebook she had found in the Blackwell house. She had only skimmed it, but there had been something about a "legacy," a mention of secrets and vengeance. She needed to read more, to see if it held any clues.

"I need to go back to the notebook," Claire said finally. "There's more in there, I'm sure of it. Something that might explain why they're so scared."

Maggie looked worried. "Are you sure that's a good idea? If they find you with that, they'll come after you again."

Claire nodded. "I know. But I don't have a choice. I need to know what my mother was looking for, what she found. It's the only way to understand what's going on."

The woman grabbed Claire's arm, her grip surprisingly strong. "Be careful," she whispered. "They're everywhere. They have people in the police, the town council, everywhere. You can't trust anyone."

Claire squeezed her hand reassuringly. "I'll be careful. But I have to do this."

Maggie stood up. "Let me help you. I can distract them, throw them off your trail."

Claire shook her head. "No, I don't want to put you in danger too. You've done enough already."

Maggie crossed her arms, her expression firm. "I'm already in danger, Claire. We both are. So, if you're going to do this, we're doing it together."

Claire smiled gratefully. "Okay. Thank you, Maggie."

Maggie nodded. "What's the plan?"

Claire thought for a moment. "We need to get to the notebook. I left it at my house. We'll need to be quick and quiet, get in and out before anyone notices."

The woman looked terrified, but she nodded. "I'll stay here. I... I can't go back out there."

Claire placed a reassuring hand on her shoulder. "Stay here and keep the door locked. We'll be back as soon as we can."

The woman nodded again, her eyes wide with fear. "Be careful."

Claire and Maggie moved quietly down the stairs and out the back door of the coffee shop, sticking to the shadows as they made their way back to Claire's house. The rain had slowed to a drizzle, but the night was still dark and ominous.

When they reached the house, Claire paused, listening for any signs of movement. The street was quiet, the house dark. She took a deep breath and moved forward, her heart pounding in her chest.

They reached the front door, and Claire quickly unlocked it, stepping inside. The house was still and silent, the air heavy with tension. She glanced around, her eyes scanning the room for any signs that someone had been there.

"Where did you leave it?" Maggie whispered.

"In the living room," Claire replied, moving toward the coffee table. The notebook was still there, right where she had left it. She grabbed it quickly and slipped it into her bag.

Just as she turned to leave, Claire heard a noise—a soft creak from upstairs. Claire froze, her breath catching in her throat. Maggie grabbed her arm, her eyes wide with fear.

"Someone's here," Maggie whispered.

Claire nodded, her heart racing. "We need to get out of here," she whispered back.

They moved toward the door, but before they could reach it, the lights flickered on. Claire's heart stopped. She turned slowly and saw a figure standing at the top of the stairs, watching them.

It was a man, tall and thin, with a shadowed face. He wore dark clothing, his eyes fixed on Claire with an intensity that sent a shiver down her spine. He didn't move, just stood there, blocking their way out.

"Who are you?" Claire demanded, her voice trembling.

The man didn't answer. Instead, he began to descend the stairs slowly, one deliberate step at a time, his eyes never leaving hers. Claire backed up, pulling Maggie with her, her mind racing.

They needed to escape before he reached them. Claire looked around, searching for another way out, her hand gripping the notebook tightly. She spotted the back door, her only chance.

"Run!" she shouted, pushing Maggie toward the door.

They bolted for the back exit, throwing it open and sprinting out into the rain. Behind them, they could hear the man's footsteps pounding against the floor, getting closer. Claire didn't dare look back, her breath coming in ragged gasps as she pushed herself harder.

They reached the car, and Claire yanked the door open, diving into the driver's seat. Maggie jumped in beside her, slamming the door shut. Claire fumbled with the keys, her hands shaking, then jammed them into the ignition.

The engine roared to life just as the man burst out of the house and ran toward them. Claire floored the gas pedal, and the car lurched forward, spraying mud and gravel as they sped away.

The man stood in the middle of the road, watching them go, his face a mask of anger. Claire glanced in the rearview mirror, her heart pounding. She had the notebook, but now they were running out of places to hide.

"We need to find out what's in this," Claire said breathlessly. "Whatever my mother found, it's in here."

Maggie nodded. "And we need to do it fast. Because whoever that was... he won't stop until he finds us."

Claire nodded, determination in her eyes. "We'll go to the one place they won't expect us to go—the old observation tower on Topsail Island."

Maggie glanced at Claire, surprised. "The observation tower? Why there?"

Claire gripped the steering wheel, her knuckles white. "Because it's abandoned. It's remote, and I remember my mother taking me there as a kid. She told me it was a place where secrets are kept safe. If she left anything for me, any clues, that's where they might be."

Maggie nodded slowly, accepting Claire's plan. "Okay, the tower it is. But we need to be careful. Whoever that was back there, he's not going to give up easily."

Claire nodded. "I know. But if we're going to end this, we need to understand what my mother found."

They drove in silence, the tension in the car thick. The rain had slowed to a drizzle, but the wind still whipped around them, the trees bending and swaying. Claire's mind raced as they made their way down the winding road toward the lighthouse, which sat on a rocky outcrop at the far end of the island, its light long extinguished.

After about twenty minutes, the road narrowed and became rougher, the trees thicker and denser. Finally, the lighthouse came into view, a tall, dark silhouette against the night sky, its once-bright beacon now dark and dead. The surrounding area was overgrown with weeds and bushes, and the path to the entrance was barely visible.

Claire parked the car behind a thick clump of trees to keep it hidden, and they got out, the cold wind biting at their skin. She grabbed the notebook from the car and tucked it under her jacket to keep it dry. Maggie shivered, pulling her coat tighter around her.

"This place gives me the creeps," Maggie muttered as they made their way toward the entrance.

"Me too," Claire admitted. "But if my mother was hiding something, this is where it would be."

They reached the base of the lighthouse, the door hanging slightly ajar. Claire pushed it open, the old hinges creaking loudly in the stillness. They stepped inside, their footsteps echoing on the cracked tile floor. The interior was cold and damp, the walls covered in peeling paint and grime. The air smelled of mildew and salt.

Maggie shined her flashlight around, revealing a narrow staircase winding up to the top of the tower. "Do you think she left something up there?"

Claire nodded. "I think it's our best bet. Let's go."

They began to climb, the steps creaking under their weight. The spiral staircase was narrow and steep, twisting upward into the darkness. Claire kept one hand on the railing, her other clutching the notebook tightly against her chest. Maggie followed close behind, her flashlight sweeping over the walls, illuminating faded graffiti and old, rusty pipes.

After what felt like an eternity, they reached the top. Claire pushed open the door to the lantern room, and they stepped inside. The room was small and circular, with large windows offering a panoramic view of the churning ocean below. The wind howled through the cracks in the glass, and the rain lashed against the panes.

Claire moved to the center of the room and set the notebook down on a small, rusted table. "We need to look through this carefully," she said. "There has to be something in here that connects all of this—my mother, Margaret Blackwell, the group, everything."

Maggie nodded, taking a deep breath. "Let's do it."

They opened the notebook together, flipping through the pages filled with Margaret Blackwell's neat, hurried handwriting. Most of the entries were about her life in the village, her work as a healer, and her fears of being accused of witchcraft. But as they neared the end, the tone of the entries shifted, becoming more urgent, more frantic.

September 15th, 1862: *I have discovered something in the marshlands, something I was not meant to find. A box, buried deep, filled with letters, records, secrets. I do not know who placed it there, but I know it is dangerous. I must hide it, keep it safe. They must never know I found it.*

Claire's heart began to race. "A box... hidden in the marshlands. Do you think it's still there?"

Maggie frowned. "If it is, that might be what your mother found. Maybe that's why they were so desperate to stop her."

Claire nodded. "We have to find it. It could hold the key to everything."

They continued flipping through the notebook, looking for more clues. Near the very end, they found another entry that made their blood run cold.

October 1st, 1862: *They are coming for me. I hear them whispering in the night, plotting against me. But I will not leave this world without a fight. I will leave a message for those who come after, a warning. My blood is in this land, and my secrets will not die with me.*

Maggie swallowed hard. "It sounds like she knew she was going to die."

Claire nodded. "She was trying to protect something, something she found. And if my mother found it too..."

Before Claire could finish, there was a loud crash from below—a door slamming open, the sound of footsteps echoing up the staircase.

"Someone's coming," Maggie whispered, her eyes wide with fear.

DARK WATERS OF TOPSAIL 51

Claire grabbed the notebook and stuffed it back under her jacket. "We need to hide," she whispered, glancing around the small room. There was nowhere to go but up, onto the narrow catwalk outside that circled the lantern room. She moved quickly to the door and pushed it open, the wind whipping her hair into her face.

"Come on," Claire urged, pulling Maggie after her.

They stepped out onto the catwalk, pressing themselves against the cold metal railing. The wind howled around them, and the rain lashed at their faces. Claire peeked through the window, trying to see who was coming up the stairs.

She saw them—a group of three men, dressed in dark clothing, moving slowly, deliberately. One of them carried a flashlight, the beam sweeping across the walls as they ascended. Claire's heart pounded in her chest. She could feel the fear coursing through her veins, but she forced herself to stay calm.

"They're coming for us," Maggie whispered, her voice barely audible over the wind.

Claire nodded. "We need to stay quiet, wait until they pass. Then we'll make a run for it."

They pressed themselves flat against the wall, the cold metal biting into their backs. The men were getting closer, their footsteps heavy on the stairs. Claire held her breath, willing herself to be still, to be silent.

Then, suddenly, the men stopped. The flashlight beam paused, and she heard one of them speak in a low, gruff voice. "I know you're up here, Claire. There's nowhere to run. Come out, and we'll make this quick."

Claire's heart skipped a beat. Maggie's hand gripped her arm tightly. "What do we do?" Maggie whispered, her voice panicked.

Claire swallowed hard, trying to think. "We wait," she whispered back. "We wait until they get closer, then we make a run for the stairs."

The men started moving again, their footsteps growing louder. Claire peeked through the window again and saw the leader's face—a hard, cold expression, his eyes scanning the room. He was only a few steps away from the top.

Claire looked at Maggie and nodded. "Now."

They moved quickly, darting around the corner of the catwalk and back into the lantern room. The men were just reaching the top of the stairs as they slipped past, heading for the staircase leading down.

"Hey!" one of the men shouted. "There they are!"

Claire didn't look back. She grabbed Maggie's hand and pulled her down the stairs, moving as fast as they could. Behind them, the men gave chase, their footsteps pounding against the metal steps.

"Go, go, go!" Claire urged, practically dragging Maggie down the narrow spiral staircase.

They reached the bottom, the door still hanging open. Claire shoved it wide and burst out into the rain, the cold air hitting her like a wall. She could hear the men shouting behind them, the sound of their footsteps growing closer.

"Run for the car!" Claire shouted, sprinting toward the trees.

Maggie followed, her breath coming in short gasps. They darted through the undergrowth, the wet branches slapping against their faces, their clothes soaked through. Claire glanced back and saw the men emerging from the watchtower, flashlights swinging wildly.

She pushed herself harder, her legs burning with effort. The car was just ahead, hidden behind the thick foliage. They reached it, and Claire yanked the door open, shoving Maggie inside. She jumped into the driver's seat and started the engine.

The headlights flared to life just as the men reached the edge of the clearing. Claire floored the gas, the tires spinning on the wet ground for a moment before catching and lurching forward.

The men shouted, one of them throwing something—a rock, a stick, Claire couldn't tell—but it missed, bouncing off the ground behind them. She drove as fast as she could, the car fishtailing on the muddy path, but she kept going, her heart racing.

They reached the main road and turned sharply, heading back toward town. Claire glanced in the rearview mirror, but the men were gone, swallowed by the darkness.

Maggie was panting, her face pale. "What now?" she asked breathlessly.

Claire gripped the wheel tighter, determination in her eyes. "We find the marshlands," "where Margaret Blackwell hid that box," Claire said, her voice firm despite the fear coursing through her veins. "Whatever she found out there, it scared those men enough to kill my mother and come after us. We need to find it before they do."

Maggie nodded, though her expression was tense. "Okay, but how do we find the exact spot? The marshlands are huge. We could be searching for days."

Claire thought for a moment, trying to recall everything she knew about the area. "The notebook," she said suddenly, reaching under her jacket and pulling it out. "Maybe Margaret left more clues in here. Something to point us in the right direction."

They continued driving as Claire flipped through the pages of the old leather-bound journal, scanning the entries carefully. The rain had stopped, but the road was still slick, the night around them dark and foreboding. Maggie kept glancing in the rearview mirror as if expecting the men to reappear at any moment.

"Here," Claire said finally, stopping on a page near the end. The handwriting was shaky, as if Margaret had written it in haste. "She talks about a tree—a great oak tree that stands alone, near the water's edge. She says it's a landmark, that it hides the entrance to something buried deep."

Maggie frowned. "A tree? In a marsh? That doesn't narrow it down much."

Claire shook her head. "No, but look—she describes it as 'the last sentinel of the forest, where the land meets the sea.' It must be near the coast, where the marshland borders the ocean."

Maggie nodded, hope sparking in her eyes. "There's only one place like that—the eastern edge of the marshlands, near where the old docks used to be. It's pretty remote, and not many people go there anymore. It's got to be what she meant."

Claire glanced at her, a determined look in her eyes. "Then that's where we're going. We just need to get there before they do."

Maggie bit her lip, then nodded. "I'll guide you. Just keep driving straight for now."

The road wound through the town and past small, darkened houses. The minutes ticked by slowly, each one weighed down by the growing tension in the car. Claire kept glancing at the notebook, hoping for more clues, but there was nothing else. Just the desperate, hurried words of a woman who had known her end was near.

They finally reached a small dirt road that branched off from the main one, barely visible in the darkness. Maggie pointed to it. "There—take that turn. It should lead us down toward the coast."

Claire turned onto the narrow path, the car bouncing over rocks and roots. The dense trees closed in around them, their branches arching overhead like a tunnel. The road twisted and turned, the headlights cutting through the gloom, but there was no sign of any other vehicles or movement.

"How much farther?" Claire asked, her voice tense.

"Not far," Maggie replied. "Just keep going until you see a clearing."

They drove for a few more minutes before the trees began to thin, and the ground became softer and wetter. The marshlands were up ahead—a wide expanse of reeds and shallow water stretching out toward the dark horizon. The sound of the ocean was faint but steady, the waves crashing softly in the distance.

Claire pulled the car to a stop at the edge of the marsh. "We'll have to go on foot from here," she said, opening the door.

Maggie got out and looked around, shivering slightly. "I don't like this place," she muttered. "It feels... wrong."

Claire nodded, feeling the same unease. The air was thick and heavy, the ground soggy beneath their feet. The marsh seemed to stretch out endlessly, dark and foreboding, with no clear paths or markers.

"We have to find that tree," Claire said, scanning the area. "It's our only chance."

They started walking, their shoes sinking into the wet earth with every step. The reeds rustled around them, whispering in the wind. Claire kept the notebook open, rereading Margaret's description, trying to match it with their surroundings.

After several minutes of searching, they came to a small rise in the ground. Ahead, silhouetted against the faint glow of the moon, stood a massive oak tree. Its branches reached out like gnarled arms, and its trunk was thick and wide, its roots plunging deep into the marshy ground.

"That must be it," Maggie whispered. "The last sentinel of the forest."

Claire felt a surge of determination. "Come on, let's go."

They hurried toward the tree, their footsteps splashing in the shallow water. As they got closer, Claire noticed something carved into the bark of the tree—a symbol, faint but visible. It looked like a series of intertwined lines, almost like a Celtic knot.

Maggie leaned in closer. "What do you think it means?"

Claire shook her head. "I don't know, but Margaret mentions symbols in her notebook... symbols that mark where things are hidden. This has to be it."

She circled the tree, scanning the ground. The oak's roots were twisted and thick, partially submerged in the water. She looked for any signs of disturbance, anything that seemed out of place.

"There," Maggie said suddenly, pointing to a spot where the ground seemed slightly raised. "Could that be it?"

Claire moved to the spot and knelt, brushing away the mud and debris with her hands. She felt something solid beneath the surface—a wooden plank. Her heart pounded as she dug deeper, uncovering more of the wood.

"It's a hatch," she whispered, excitement rising in her voice. "Help me get it open."

Maggie crouched beside her, and together they pried at the edges of the wooden hatch. It was old and rotting, but after a few minutes, it began to give way, creaking as they lifted it.

Underneath, they found a small, dark hole, just big enough for a person to climb through. Claire shined her flashlight down, revealing a narrow tunnel that seemed to lead underground.

"This must be it," Claire said, her voice a mixture of fear and excitement. "The entrance Margaret mentioned."

Maggie looked uneasy. "Are you sure about this?"

Claire nodded. "We've come this far. We can't turn back now."

She climbed down into the hole, gripping the edges of the tunnel for support. The walls were damp and slick, the air cold and musty. Maggie followed, and together they descended into the darkness.

The tunnel was cramped and narrow, just wide enough for them to move single-file. The ground sloped downward, and the air grew colder with every step. Claire kept her flashlight trained ahead, her heart pounding in her chest.

After what felt like an eternity, they reached the end of the tunnel and emerged into a small, underground chamber. The room was filled with old, wooden crates and boxes, stacked haphazardly against the walls. In the center of the room was a large, metal chest, half-buried in the dirt.

"This has to be it," Claire said, moving toward the chest.

She knelt down and brushed away the dirt, revealing a heavy metal lock. She felt around the edges, looking for a way to open it. Maggie watched nervously, glancing back toward the tunnel.

Claire found a latch and pulled it. The lock gave way with a loud click, and the lid of the chest creaked open. Inside, they found a collection of old, yellowed papers, letters, and a few leather-bound journals.

Claire's hands trembled as she lifted one of the journals out, opening it to the first page. The handwriting was neat and precise, unmistakably her mother's.

"It's her journal," Claire whispered, her voice catching in her throat. "My mother's... she was here. She knew about this."

Maggie leaned over, peering at the pages. "What does it say?"

Claire flipped through the journal, skimming the entries. Her mother had written extensively about her search for Margaret Blackwell's secrets, detailing everything she had discovered—the curse, the strange group in the town, and finally, the box hidden in the marshlands.

May 14th, 2022: *I found it. The box Margaret hid so long ago, filled with letters and records, evidence of everything they've done. It's all here—the truth about the disappearances, about the group, about what they've been hiding. I need to be careful. They know I'm close. They're watching me. But I have to expose them, for Claire... for everyone.*

Tears filled Claire's eyes as she read her mother's words. "She found it," she whispered. "She found the proof... the proof they were hiding."

Maggie glanced around nervously. "We need to get out of here, Claire. If they find us—"

Before she could finish, there was a noise from the tunnel—a faint, echoing sound, like footsteps.

Claire's head snapped up. "They're coming."

Maggie's eyes widened in fear. "What do we do?"

Claire quickly shoved the journal into her jacket and looked around for an escape. "There must be another way out. We have to find it—now!"

They began searching the chamber, moving crates and boxes aside. Claire's heart pounded in her chest, her hands shaking with fear. The footsteps grew louder and closer, echoing through the narrow tunnel.

Then, in the corner of the chamber, Maggie found a small, hidden door, partially covered by a stack of old crates. "Here!" she whispered urgently. "

"Help me move these," Maggie urged, her voice tense.

Claire rushed over, and together, they shoved the crates aside, revealing a narrow wooden door, weathered and cracked but intact. The footsteps in the tunnel were growing louder, the sounds of their pursuers drawing closer with every passing second. Claire's hands were trembling, but she forced herself to stay focused.

She grabbed the handle and yanked the door open. It creaked loudly, and for a moment, Claire feared it would break, but it held. Beyond the door, she could see another tunnel, this one narrower and darker than the first, but it led away from their current position.

"Come on!" Claire whispered, pulling Maggie through the door behind her.

They slipped into the tunnel, and Claire shut the door as quietly as she could, trying not to make any noise. The tunnel was cramped, barely wide enough for them to walk side by side, and the air was colder, mustier. She switched off her flashlight, afraid that the light would give them away, and they moved forward in near-total darkness.

The sound of footsteps was muffled now, but they could still hear them, echoing faintly through the walls of the chamber they had just left. Claire felt her heart hammering in her chest, fear threatening to overwhelm her, but she pushed it down, forcing herself to focus on moving forward, one step at a time.

The tunnel seemed to twist and turn, leading them deeper underground. Claire could feel the dampness clinging to her skin, the air growing colder with every step. Her hand brushed against the rough stone wall, and she kept it there, using it as a guide. Maggie was right beside her, her breathing quick and shallow.

"What if they find us?" Maggie whispered, barely audible.

"They won't," Claire replied, though she wasn't sure if she believed it herself. "We just need to keep moving. There has to be a way out."

They continued, the tunnel gradually sloping upward. Claire felt a flicker of hope. Maybe this tunnel would lead them to the surface, away from their pursuers. The air grew slightly fresher, and she thought she could hear the faint sound of water—maybe the marsh or a nearby stream.

Then, suddenly, there was a faint light ahead—a soft, bluish glow that seemed to come from around a bend in the tunnel. Claire paused, unsure whether to be relieved or afraid. Maggie gripped her arm.

"What is it?" Maggie whispered.

"I don't know," Claire replied, her voice low. "But it's our only way out. Let's go."

They moved cautiously toward the light, their footsteps silent on the damp ground. As they rounded the corner, the tunnel opened into a larger underground chamber, and they could see the source of the light—an old, rusted lantern hanging from a hook on the wall, flickering weakly. The chamber was partially filled with water, the ground uneven and muddy.

Claire and Maggie exchanged a glance. "Someone's been here," Maggie said, her voice tense.

"Recently," Claire added, feeling a prickle of fear. She looked around the chamber, searching for any sign of movement. There were footprints in the mud—large, booted prints leading in and out of the chamber. Whoever had left the lantern was close.

"We need to keep moving," Claire whispered, guiding Maggie across the muddy ground.

They edged along the chamber's wall, moving toward the far side where another tunnel seemed to lead upward. But just as they reached it, there was a splash behind them, followed by the sound of footsteps entering the chamber. Claire turned sharply, and in the faint glow of the lantern, she saw two of the men from the watchtower—dark clothes, serious expressions, and a determination that sent a chill through her bones.

"There they are!" one of them shouted, pointing.

"Run!" Claire yelled, pulling Maggie toward the exit.

They sprinted for the tunnel, their feet slipping in the mud, the men's shouts echoing behind them. Claire could hear their pursuers splashing through the water, their footsteps pounding against the muddy ground. She and Maggie ducked into the narrow tunnel, racing upward, the walls closing in around them.

The tunnel was steep and rough, the ceiling low enough that they had to crouch as they ran. Claire's lungs burned, her legs aching with every step, but she kept going, urging Maggie on. She could hear the men getting closer, their breathing heavy, their footsteps relentless.

The tunnel took a sharp turn to the right, and suddenly, they emerged into a small, open space. Claire paused, her heart pounding, and realized they were outside again, under the open sky. They had come out on the far side of the marsh, near a narrow stream that wound its way through the reeds.

Maggie gasped, catching her breath. "What now?" she asked, fear in her eyes.

"We keep going," Claire replied, scanning the area. "We have to put as much distance between us and them as we can. Come on."

They took off again, running along the edge of the stream, the ground soft and slippery beneath their feet. The reeds swayed in the wind, and the distant sound of the ocean, the waves crashing against the shore, was louder now.

Behind them, they could still hear the men, their voices faint but growing louder as they closed in. Claire felt panic rising in her chest.

She didn't know how much longer they could keep running, but she knew they had to try.

Then, up ahead, she saw a small wooden bridge spanning the stream, leading to a narrow trail that wound through the marsh. It looked old and rickety, but it was their only option.

"This way!" Claire shouted, leading Maggie toward the bridge.

They reached the bridge just as the men emerged from the tunnel behind them, their shouts growing louder. Claire and Maggie scrambled across the wooden planks, the bridge swaying under their weight. The wood creaked and groaned, but it held.

They reached the other side and kept running, following the trail as it wound deeper into the marsh. The reeds grew taller, the ground softer. Claire's breath came in ragged gasps, her legs burning with effort.

Finally, after what felt like hours, they reached a small clearing sheltered by a thick cluster of trees. Claire stopped, leaning against a tree trunk, trying to catch her breath. Maggie collapsed beside her, her face pale and streaked with mud.

"Did we lose them?" Maggie whispered, glancing back.

Claire listened for a moment, her heart still racing. The men's shouts were distant now, fading into the sounds of the marsh. She nodded slowly. "I think so. At least for now."

They both sank to the ground, exhausted. Claire pulled out the journal, opening it again, her fingers still trembling. "We need to figure out what's in here," she said. "Whatever my mother found... it's in these pages. We need to understand it before they find us again."

Maggie nodded, her face determined despite her fear. "Then let's find out."

They sat in the clearing, huddled together, as they began to read. The journal was filled with detailed notes, names, dates, descriptions of meetings, letters, and documents. It described the strange rituals and activities of the secret group that had been protecting the town's dark secrets for generations.

Claire turned to the last few pages and found her mother's final entry.

May 30th, 2022: *They're coming for me. I know too much, and they won't let me leave. But I have to protect Claire. If you're reading this, sweetheart, find the box, find the letters. Everything you need to expose them is there. Don't be afraid. You have the strength I never did. Trust yourself, and know that I love you, always.*

Tears welled up in Claire's eyes as she read her mother's words. "She was trying to protect me," Claire whispered. "She knew they were coming for her."

Maggie put a comforting hand on her shoulder. "She wanted you to know the truth, Claire. And now we have to finish what she started."

Claire nodded, determination hardening in her chest. "We have to get these letters out. We need to show the world what's been happening here, what they've been hiding. We need to expose them, once and for all."

Maggie nodded. "But how? We can't trust the local police, and we don't know how many people are involved."

Claire thought for a moment. "We go to the press. Someone outside this town, someone who won't be afraid to dig deep and tell the truth. We find a reporter—someone who can help us get this story out there."

Maggie nodded. "That's a good plan. But first, we need to get out of here."

Claire closed the journal and stood up, her resolve firm. "Let's go. We're not stopping until we find justice for my mother... and for everyone else they've hurt."

They started back toward the trail, ready to face whatever came next, knowing they were no longer running away but toward the truth.

Chapter 8
The Trap

Claire and Maggie moved cautiously through the thick marshland, the reeds whispering around them in the wind. Their feet squelched on the soft ground, water seeping into their shoes with every step. The air was heavy with moisture, and the faint smell of salt from the ocean hung in the air.

As they pressed forward, Claire kept glancing behind them, listening for any sign of pursuit. The men had seemed to lose their trail, but she couldn't shake the feeling that they were being watched, that eyes were tracking their every move from the darkness. She kept the journal tucked securely inside her jacket as if it were a talisman that could protect them.

Maggie broke the silence. "Do you really think we'll be able to find a reporter who will believe us? Who won't think we're just two crazy women with a wild story?"

Claire nodded, determination set in her eyes. "I think it's our only shot. We have the proof now, the journal, the letters, the names. If we can find the right person, someone who's not afraid to dig into this, we can blow the lid off everything they've been hiding."

Maggie glanced around nervously. "But how do we get to a reporter without them finding us first? They have eyes everywhere."

Claire took a deep breath. "We'll need to get to Wilmington. It's the nearest big city, and I know a journalist there—*Sarah Whitaker*. She's always been interested in local stories, especially ones that uncover corruption. She'll listen to us, I'm sure of it."

Maggie nodded, but Claire could see the fear in her friend's eyes. "How do we get there without being caught?"

"We'll have to be smart," Claire replied. "And careful. We can't use our phones; they might be tracking us. We'll take back roads and keep off the main routes. We'll need to get supplies, find some cash, and move fast."

Maggie's eyes widened. "And what if they're already on their way to Wilmington, waiting for us?"

Claire set her jaw. "Then we'll find another way. But we can't stay here. We're too exposed."

They reached the edge of the marsh, where a small road cut through the landscape. Claire looked both ways, making sure the coast was clear. "Come on," she said. "We'll head to the gas station just outside town. If we're lucky, we can get a ride or find some way to disappear for a while."

They crossed the road quickly and slipped into the cover of the woods on the other side, keeping low and moving fast. The trees were thick here, their branches hanging low, casting deep shadows across the ground. Claire felt her adrenaline kicking in, every nerve on high alert.

The gas station was a small, run-down place at the edge of Topsail, a relic from another time. A single dim light flickered over the pumps, and the sign above the door swung creakily in the wind. Claire and Maggie approached cautiously, scanning the area for any sign of the men who had been chasing them.

Inside, a tired-looking clerk was reading a magazine behind the counter, and a single pickup truck was parked out front. Claire motioned for Maggie to stay back while she entered. The bell above the door jingled, and the clerk looked up, his expression bored.

"Can I help you?" he asked, barely glancing at her.

Claire smiled, trying to keep her voice calm. "Yeah, I'm just passing through. Do you know if there's a bus station nearby?"

The clerk snorted. "Not around here. The nearest one is in Wilmington."

Claire nodded. "Figures. Thanks anyway."

She turned to leave when she caught sight of a notice board by the door. Among the various flyers and announcements was a handwritten note: *"Rideshare to Wilmington—Call Jim at 555-4892."* Claire's heart skipped a beat.

She tore the note off the board and hurried back outside to Maggie. "I found something," she whispered. "There's a guy offering rides to Wilmington. It's not much, but it's a start."

Maggie glanced around nervously. "How do we know it's safe?"

Claire shrugged. "We don't. But we don't have a lot of options right now. We'll have to take the risk."

They walked a short distance from the gas station to a nearby payphone, one of the few relics still left in the small town. Claire quickly dialed the number, her heart racing as she waited for an answer. After a few rings, a gruff voice came on the line.

"Yeah, who's this?"

"Hi, is this Jim?" Claire asked, trying to keep her voice steady.

"Yeah, who's asking?"

"I saw your note at the gas station. I'm looking for a ride to Wilmington. Are you still heading that way?"

There was a pause on the other end. "Maybe. Depends. You got cash?"

"Yes, I can pay," Claire replied quickly.

"Alright," Jim said. "Meet me behind the old boatyard in fifteen minutes. Don't be late."

Before Claire could say anything else, he hung up. She turned to Maggie, her face serious. "We need to get to the boatyard. It's not far, but we don't have much time."

Maggie nodded, and they set off quickly, moving through the shadows. The boatyard was a few blocks away, down by the water's edge. It was abandoned now, a crumbling shell of a place that had once been busy with fishermen and their boats.

They reached the edge of the boatyard just as a rusted pickup truck pulled up, its headlights off. A man with a scruffy beard and a baseball cap leaned out of the driver's window, squinting at them in the dark.

"You the ones looking for a ride?" he asked.

Claire nodded. "Yeah. Are you Jim?"

The man nodded. "That's me. Hop in the back. We need to get moving."

Claire and Maggie exchanged a wary glance but climbed into the back of the truck. Jim hit the gas, and the truck bounced down the dirt road, heading away from the boatyard and toward the highway.

As they drove, Claire felt a flicker of hope. Maybe they had gotten lucky. Maybe they would make it to Wilmington after all. She kept one hand on the journal inside her jacket, feeling its weight against her chest, a reminder of why they were doing this.

But as the truck picked up speed, Claire noticed something in the side mirror: a pair of headlights following them at a distance. Her stomach tightened. Were they being followed?

She leaned closer to the window, trying to get a better look. The headlights were getting closer, the car behind them speeding up to match their pace. Claire's heart began to race. "Jim," she called over the wind, "are you expecting anyone else on this road?"

Jim glanced in the rearview mirror, his face darkening. "No. Why?"

"Because someone's following us," Claire said, her voice tense.

Jim cursed under his breath and slammed his foot on the gas. The truck lurched forward, speeding down the road. Claire and Maggie held on tight, the wind whipping around them as they raced through the darkness.

The car behind them accelerated, too, closing the distance. Claire's mind raced, fear spiking through her. Had they been set up? Had Jim been working with their pursuers all along?

"Hold on!" Jim shouted, swerving the truck onto a narrow side road, tires screeching. The truck skidded across the gravel, bouncing over potholes as they took a sharp turn.

Claire glanced back again; the car was still behind them, its headlights blinding in the darkness. "They're not giving up," she muttered, panic rising in her chest.

Jim's face was set, his jaw clenched. "I'll lose them," he grunted. "Hang on."

The road twisted and turned, winding through thick woods. Jim took another sharp turn, then another, trying to shake their pursuers. The car behind them struggled to keep up, its headlights weaving erratically.

For a moment, it seemed like they might lose them, but then Jim suddenly slammed on the brakes, the truck screeching to a halt. "Get out!" he shouted.

"What? Why?" Claire asked, confused.

"Out!" Jim barked. "Now!"

Claire and Maggie scrambled out of the truck, fear gripping them. Jim hit the gas again, speeding away without another word, leaving them standing on the side of the road.

"What the hell was that?" Maggie whispered, panic in her voice.

Claire's eyes darted around. "I don't know," Claire muttered, her mind racing. "But I don't think we can trust anyone right now."

Maggie's breathing was rapid, her eyes wide with fear. "What do we do, Claire? Where are we?"

Claire glanced around, trying to get her bearings. They were on a narrow, deserted road surrounded by dense woods, the trees pressing in like a dark wall on either side. The air was thick with humidity, and she could barely see through the darkness.

"We need to get off the road," Claire said, grabbing Maggie's arm and pulling her toward the tree line. "If they're still following us, they'll look here first."

They slipped into the woods, crouching low as they made their way deeper into the undergrowth. The forest sounds surrounded them: leaves rustling, branches cracking underfoot, and the distant hoot of an owl. Claire's heart pounded in her chest as she tried to stay quiet, her ears straining for any sign of the men who had been chasing them.

After a few tense minutes, they heard it: the low rumble of an engine approaching. Claire and Maggie dropped to the ground, pressing themselves flat against the damp earth, trying to stay hidden. The car's headlights swept across the road, illuminating the trees for a brief moment before moving on.

Claire held her breath, watching as the car slowed, its engine idling, the driver searching. She could barely make out two figures inside, but the car's high beams were blinding, making it hard to see any details.

After what felt like an eternity, the car started moving again, creeping slowly down the road, its headlights flickering through the trees. Claire didn't dare move until the sound of the engine faded into the distance. She glanced at Maggie, who looked just as terrified as she felt.

"We have to keep moving," Claire whispered, her voice barely audible. "If they find us out here, we're done for."

Maggie nodded, swallowing hard. "Do you think Jim set us up?"

Claire frowned, considering. "I don't know. He might have been trying to help, but he knew more than he let on. We can't risk going back to town now; they'll be watching the roads."

Maggie took a deep breath. "So, where do we go?"

Claire thought for a moment, then said, "There's an old trail that leads back to the coast, near the marshlands. It's not far from here. If we can make it to the shoreline, we might be able to find a boat or a place to hide until morning."

Maggie nodded again. "Okay, let's go. But we have to be careful."

They moved carefully through the woods, staying low and sticking close to the trees. The ground was uneven and slippery, the thick undergrowth clawing at their clothes as they pressed forward. Claire kept her eyes focused ahead, every sense on high alert. She could feel the fear and adrenaline coursing through her veins, but she pushed it down, concentrating on the path ahead.

After what felt like hours, they emerged from the woods onto a narrow trail, barely visible in the dark. The moon was hidden behind thick clouds, and they had to rely on the faint glow of the stars and the sounds of the waves to guide them. The trail sloped downward, leading toward the distant sound of crashing waves.

As they descended, the wind picked up, carrying the salty tang of the ocean. Claire's heart lifted slightly at the familiar scent; they were getting closer. The trail wound around a small hill, and soon, they could see the water ahead, the dark, choppy surface stretching out like a vast, endless expanse.

"We made it," Maggie whispered, relief in her voice. "Now what?"

Claire scanned the shoreline, looking for any sign of a boat or a place to hide. The shoreline was rocky, with large tree stumps scattered along the water's edge. There was an old dock in the distance, partially collapsed, but she couldn't see any boats.

"Let's check the dock," Claire suggested, moving quickly toward it. "Maybe there's something we can use."

They hurried across the rocky shoreline, the wind whipping their hair and the waves crashing loudly against the shore. When they reached the dock, Claire saw that it was in worse shape than she had thought—wooden planks rotting and broken, parts of it submerged in the water.

Maggie frowned. "Are you sure about this? It doesn't look safe."

Claire bit her lip. "I know, but we don't have many options. We need to keep moving."

They stepped carefully onto the dock, the wood creaking and groaning under their weight. The wind was stronger here, the waves splashing against the posts, sending sprays of cold water up into the air.

Claire moved slowly, testing each step before putting her full weight down.

About halfway down the dock, she spotted something: a small motorboat tied loosely to one of the remaining posts. It looked old and battered, but it was intact.

"There," Claire said, pointing. "If we can get that boat started, we might be able to make it up the ICW to Wilmington or at least find somewhere safer."

Maggie looked skeptical. "Do you know how to drive that thing?"

Claire managed a faint smile. "I grew up here, remember? My dad taught me when I was a kid. I think I can manage."

They reached the boat, and Claire quickly untied it, pulling the rope free. She climbed in and checked the fuel gauge; there was still some gas left, not much, but hopefully enough to get them to safety. She turned the ignition, and after a few tense seconds, the engine sputtered to life.

Maggie climbed in beside her, and Claire pushed off from the dock, steering the boat away from the shore. The small craft rocked and bounced on the waves, but Claire kept a firm grip on the wheel, guiding them out into deeper water.

"We did it," Maggie said, a hint of relief in her voice. "We're getting away."

But before Claire could respond, she heard a distant roar growing louder. She looked over her shoulder and saw a set of headlights on the shore, a car speeding toward the dock.

"They found us," Claire muttered, her fear spiking again.

The car skidded to a stop, and two figures jumped out, running toward the edge of the dock. Claire turned the boat sharply, pushing the throttle as far as it would go. The engine roared, and the boat surged forward, skimming over the waves.

Shots rang out behind them, bullets zipping past and splashing into the water. Maggie ducked down, covering her head. "Claire, go faster!" she shouted, panic in her voice.

"I'm trying!" Claire shouted back, her hands gripping the wheel tightly. The boat bounced violently on the waves, the engine whining with effort. She could hear the men shouting on the shore, their voices faint but filled with anger.

They sped out into the ICW, putting distance between themselves and the shore. Claire glanced back and saw the men standing at the edge of the dock, their silhouettes framed by the car's headlights.

"We're not out of this yet," Claire muttered, focusing on the horizon.

Maggie peeked over the side, her face pale. "Do you think they'll follow us?"

Claire shook her head. "I don't know. But if they have a boat of their own, they might try. We need to keep moving, stay ahead of them."

They continued pushing through the waves, the wind howling around them. The coastline was barely visible in the dark, just a shadowy outline against the sky. Claire kept her eyes on the water, scanning for any sign of another boat, any indication that they were still being chased.

Minutes turned into an hour, and still, there was no sign of pursuit. Vast and dark, the water stretched out around them. The only sound was the roar of the engine and the crashing of the waves. Claire began to relax just a little, a tiny flicker of hope igniting her chest.

"We might have lost them," she said quietly.

Maggie sat up, shivering from the cold. "Where are we heading?"

"Toward Wilmington," Claire replied. "We'll keep going until we find a safe place to dock. From there, we'll find Sarah Whitaker and get this story out."

Maggie nodded, though she still looked worried. "I just hope we have enough gas to get there."

Claire nodded, feeling the weight of their situation. "Me too."

They continued, the boat cutting through the water, Wilmington still miles away. The wind was picking up again, the waves growing choppier. Claire's hands ached from gripping the wheel, but she didn't dare let go.

Then, out of the corner of her eye, she saw something, a dark shape moving across the water, far in the distance. Her heart sank. She squinted, trying to make it out.

Maggie noticed her tension. "What is it?"

Claire's voice was grim. "I think... I think there's another boat."

Maggie turned, her eyes widening. "Are you sure?"

Claire nodded slowly, dread creeping up her spine. "I'm sure. And they're coming right at us."

Shots rang out behind them, bullets zipping past and splashing into the water. Maggie ducked down, covering her head. "Claire, go faster!" she shouted, panic in her voice.

"I'm trying!" Claire shouted back, her hands gripping the wheel tightly. The boat bounced violently on the waves, the engine whining with effort. She could hear the men shouting on the shore, their voices faint but filled with anger.

They sped out into the ICW, putting distance between themselves and the shore. Claire glanced back and saw the men standing at the edge of the dock, their silhouettes framed by the car's headlights.

"We're not out of this yet," Claire muttered, focusing on the horizon.

Maggie peeked over the side, her face pale. "Do you think they'll follow us?"

Claire shook her head. "I don't know. But if they have a boat of their own, they might try. We need to keep moving, stay ahead of them."

They continued pushing through the waves, the wind howling around them. The coastline was barely visible in the dark, just a shadowy outline against the sky. Claire kept her eyes on the water, scanning for any sign of another boat, any indication that they were still being chased.

Minutes turned into an hour, and still, there was no sign of pursuit. Vast and dark, the water stretched out around them. The only sound was the roar of the engine and the crashing of the waves. Claire began to relax just a little, a tiny flicker of hope igniting her chest.

"We might have lost them," she said quietly.

Maggie sat up, shivering from the cold. "Where are we heading?"

"Toward Wilmington," Claire replied. "We'll keep going until we find a safe place to dock. From there, we'll find Sarah Whitaker and get this story out."

Maggie nodded, though she still looked worried. "I just hope we have enough gas to get there."

Claire nodded, feeling the weight of their situation. "Me too."

They continued, the boat cutting through the water, Wilmington still miles away. The wind was picking up again, the waves growing choppier. Claire's hands ached from gripping the wheel, but she didn't dare let go.

Then, out of the corner of her eye, she saw something, a dark shape moving across the water, far in the distance. Her heart sank. She squinted, trying to make it out.

Maggie noticed her tension. "What is it?"

Claire's voice was grim. "I think... I think there's another boat."

Maggie turned, her eyes widening. "Are you sure?"

Claire nodded slowly, dread creeping up her spine. "I'm sure. And they're coming right at us."

Chapter 9
The Pursuit

The dark shape on the horizon grew larger, the faint outline of a boat becoming clearer with every second. Claire's heart hammered in her chest as she tightened her grip on the wheel. The approaching boat was moving fast, too fast to be just a coincidence. Whoever was on board was coming straight for them.

Maggie turned to Claire, her voice a tight whisper. "What do we do, Claire? If they catch us..."

Claire didn't hesitate. "We won't let them catch us. Hold on!" She pushed the throttle forward, coaxing every ounce of speed from the small motorboat. The engine roared louder, and the boat surged forward, cutting through the waves. The wind whipped at their faces, cold and sharp, the salt spray stinging their skin.

She glanced back over her shoulder. The other boat was closer now, its silhouette clearer against the dark water. It was bigger than theirs and faster, too, a powerful craft designed for speed. Claire felt a jolt of fear but forced herself to stay focused. She had grown up on these waters; she knew how to navigate the currents, the hidden sandbars, and the shoals. She just had to keep them moving to find a way to lose their pursuers.

Maggie clung to the side of the boat, her face pale. "Can we outrun them?" she shouted over the roar of the wind and the engine.

Claire shook her head, her eyes fixed on the horizon. "No, but I know these waters better than they do. I'll take us through the shallows; they won't risk running aground if they're smart."

She veered to the right, steering them closer to the shoreline. The waves grew rougher and choppier, and she had to fight to keep the boat steady. She knew the shallows well; the water was treacherous here, full of hidden sandbanks and downed trees. If she could get them close enough, the other boat might be forced to slow down or take a different route.

The pursuing boat didn't waver. Claire could hear its engine now, a deep, throaty growl that carried over the wind. She glanced back again, her stomach tightening as she saw it gaining on them, cutting through the water with relentless speed.

"Come on, come on," she muttered to herself, turning the wheel sharply. She guided their boat closer to the shore, where the water was shallower. She could see the white froth of waves breaking over hidden sandbars. The boat jolted as it skimmed over a submerged branch, but Claire kept her grip firm, steering them through the narrow channel.

Behind them, the larger boat hesitated, its driver clearly aware of the danger. Claire allowed herself a flicker of hope; if they could just get a little farther, they might be able to lose them in the maze of shallows.

But the hope was short-lived. The pursuing boat slowed only for a moment, then picked up speed again, heading straight for them. The driver must have realized they were desperate and were taking the risk.

Maggie's eyes widened. "They're not stopping! They're going to follow us through!"

Claire gritted her teeth, adrenaline surging through her veins. "Then we'll have to make it harder for them."

She twisted the wheel, turning sharply to the left, bringing them even closer to the shoreline. The boat bounced and rocked on the waves, the engine sputtering with the strain. Claire's hands were numb from the cold, but she kept going, her eyes scanning the water for the safest route.

The larger boat was almost upon them now, so close that Claire could see the figures on board, two men dressed in dark clothing, their faces shadowed by the moonlight. One of them raised an arm, pointing straight at them.

"They're getting closer!" Maggie shouted, panic creeping into her voice.

"I know!" Claire shouted back. She spotted a narrow passage ahead, barely wide enough for their small boat. It led between two large trees, where the water was even shallower. It was a risky move, but it was their best chance. "Hold on tight!"

She gunned the engine, steering them straight for the passage. The boat skimmed over the waves, the hull scraping against a submerged tree. Maggie let out a small yelp, but Claire kept going, threading the needle between the rocks.

Behind them, the larger boat hesitated again, and Claire saw one of the men shouting, pointing wildly. The driver of the pursuing boat tried to turn, but it was too late. The boat hit a hidden sandbank with a loud crunch, its hull grinding against the sandy bottom.

"They're stuck!" Maggie exclaimed, relief flooding her voice.

Claire didn't waste a second. She pushed the throttle harder, speeding through the narrow passage and out into the water on the other side. The pursuing boat was still stuck, its engine roaring as the driver tried to free it.

"We did it!" Maggie cheered, her face lighting up with hope. "We lost them!"

Claire nodded, but her expression remained tense. "For now. But they'll find a way to get free, and they'll come after us again. We need to keep moving."

She kept the boat at full speed, heading away from the shallows and back out into deeper water. The shoreline stretched out ahead of them, dark and foreboding, but it offered some safety. If they could make it far enough, they might reach Wilmington before their pursuers caught up.

Minutes passed like hours as they sped across the water, the boat's engine straining. Claire kept checking, searching for any sign of the other boat. The tension was almost unbearable, but she pushed it down, focusing on the task at hand.

Finally, Maggie spoke again, her voice calmer. "Do you think they're really after Margaret Blackwell's secret? The truth your mother found?"

Claire nodded, her jaw tight. "I think so. Whatever she discovered, it was big enough to scare them. Big enough that they'd kill to keep it hidden."

Maggie shivered, glancing back at the dark water. "What could be so important that they'd go to these lengths?"

Claire shook her head. "I don't know. But I intend to find out."

They continued on, the shoreline creeping closer, the lights of Wilmington barely visible in the distance. Claire felt a surge of hope—maybe, just maybe, they were going to make it.

But then she saw a flash of light on the water behind them. Her heart sank as she realized what it was. The other boat, now free from the sandbank, was back in pursuit. And it was gaining on them fast.

"They're back!" Maggie shouted, panic in her voice.

Claire swore under her breath, her eyes narrowing. "We're almost to Wilmington. We just need a little more time. Hold on!"

She pushed the throttle to its limit, the engine roaring in protest. The boat leaped forward, racing toward the distant lights. The pursuing boat was closing in, its larger engine giving it an advantage, but Claire was determined not to give up.

The water grew choppier as they approached the mouth of the Cape Fear River, the current pulling at the boat. Claire fought to keep them steady, her muscles aching with the effort. The other boat was almost upon them, its bow slicing through the waves like a knife.

"We're not going to make it!" Maggie shouted, fear in her eyes.

"Yes, we will!" Claire yelled back, though doubt gnawed at her. She scanned the shoreline, searching for any sign of help.

Then, up ahead, she saw a small pier jutting out into the water, a lone figure standing at the end, waving a flashlight.

"There!" Claire shouted, steering the boat toward the pier. "Someone's there! Maybe they can help us!"

Maggie nodded, clinging to the side of the boat. "Go! Hurry!"

Claire pushed the boat harder, the engine roaring as they raced toward the pier. The figure on the dock waved more frantically, the flashlight beam cutting through the dark.

The pursuing boat was almost on top of them now, its engine roaring like a beast. Claire could see the men on board, their faces set with grim determination. She had seconds, maybe less, before they caught up.

She steered hard to the left, bringing them alongside the pier. The figure on the dock, a man in a hooded raincoat, reached out, shouting something she couldn't hear over the roar of the wind and the water.

"Jump!" Claire yelled to Maggie. "Now!"

Maggie hesitated for only a moment, then leaped from the boat, landing hard on the pier. Claire followed, grabbing the outstretched hand of the man in the raincoat. He pulled her up just as the pursuing boat came crashing into the dock, wood splintering on impact.

"Run!" the man shouted, his voice urgent. "They're right behind you!"

Claire didn't wait to ask questions. She grabbed Maggie's arm, and they sprinted down the pier toward the shore, the sound of their pursuers scrambling after them.

She didn't know who this man was or why he was helping them, but she knew one thing: they were out of time, and the only way to survive was to keep running.

Chapter 10
The Escape

Claire's heart pounded as she and Maggie sprinted down the narrow pier, the wooden planks creaking beneath their feet. Behind them, the men shouted, their footsteps heavy and fast. The man in the hooded raincoat ran beside them, his face partially obscured but his voice urgent.

"This way!" he yelled, motioning toward a small path leading away from the pier and into a cluster of thick trees.

Claire didn't hesitate. She pulled Maggie along, following the stranger into the dark. The sounds of their pursuers grew louder, the crunch of boots on wood echoing behind them. The path was narrow and overgrown, branches slapping against their faces, but Claire kept moving, adrenaline coursing through her veins.

They reached the cover of the trees, and the man in the raincoat led them into the shadows, weaving through the dense foliage with practiced ease. Claire glanced back over her shoulder, trying to catch a glimpse of their pursuers, but the darkness was thick, and the men had not yet reached the tree line.

The man stopped suddenly, grabbing Claire's arm. "Keep low," he whispered. "Follow me, and don't make a sound."

Claire nodded, gripping Maggie's hand tighter. They crouched low and moved through the undergrowth, the cold, damp earth seeping through their shoes. The man led them deeper into the woods, away from the pier and the water, and soon, the sounds of their pursuers faded into the distance.

After several minutes, they reached a small clearing, partially hidden by a cluster of thick pines. The man stopped and turned to face them, his breath heavy. "We should be safe here for a moment," he whispered. "At least until they pass."

Claire nodded, her breath coming in sharp, shallow gasps. "Who are you?" she asked, her voice low but insistent. "Why are you helping us?"

The man pulled back his hood, revealing a weathered face and a pair of sharp, intelligent eyes. "Name's *Ethan Cole*," he said. "I'm a journalist. I've been following these guys for months."

Claire's eyes widened. "A journalist? Are you with *Sarah Whitaker*?"

Ethan nodded, a faint smile touching his lips. "Sarah's a friend. She tipped me off when she heard about your mother's death and told me there might be a bigger story here. Looks like she was right."

Maggie looked skeptical. "How did you know where to find us?"

Ethan shrugged. "I've been trailing those men since they got here. Figured they were looking for someone, and when I saw you out on the water, I knew you had to be it."

Claire felt a flicker of hope. "Then you know what's going on? You know about the group?"

Ethan's expression grew serious. "I know enough to be worried. These guys... they're dangerous. They've been pulling the strings in this town for a long time, keeping secrets buried. And from what I've gathered, your mother got too close to something they didn't want anyone to know."

Claire nodded, pulling the journal from her jacket. "My mother left this. It has names, dates, and details about what they were hiding. I think it's the key to exposing them."

Ethan's eyes widened as he took the journal, flipping through the pages quickly. "This... this could be huge," he muttered. "But we need more. We need to get this to Sarah to get it out there before they catch up to us."

Maggie glanced back in the direction of the pier. "Do you think we lost them?"

Ethan shook his head. "Not for long. They're relentless. But I've got a car nearby. We can make a run for it, get to Wilmington before they figure out where we've gone."

Claire nodded. "Okay, let's go. We don't have much time."

Ethan led them out of the clearing, keeping low as they moved through the woods. The terrain was uneven, filled with roots and brambles, but they kept going, driven by the urgency of their situation. Claire's mind raced with everything that had happened: the men, the chase, and the truth hidden in her mother's journal. She felt a surge of determination. They had to make it. They had to expose this.

After about ten minutes, they reached a small dirt road. A car was parked there, a nondescript sedan with its lights off. Ethan hurried to the driver's side and unlocked the doors.

"Get in," he urged.

Claire and Maggie climbed into the back, and Ethan slid into the driver's seat. He started the engine, the headlights flaring to life, and drove down the road, taking care to keep his speed steady and not draw attention.

"We'll take the back roads," Ethan said, his eyes scanning the darkness. "It'll take longer, but it's safer."

Claire nodded, glancing at Maggie, who looked pale but determined. "Thank you," she said quietly. "For helping us."

Ethan glanced at her in the rearview mirror, a small smile on his lips. "I'm not doing it just for you. If what's in that journal is true, this could be the story of a lifetime. And I want to see those bastards pay for what they've done."

They drove in silence for a while, the road winding through thick woods. The only sounds were the engine's hum and the occasional rustle of leaves in the wind. Claire kept her eyes on the road, watching for any sign of pursuit.

After about an hour, they reached the outskirts of Wilmington. The city lights glittered in the distance, a beacon of hope. Ethan took a deep breath and slowed the car as they approached a more populated area.

"We're almost there," he said. "Sarah's office is just a few blocks away. She'll know what to do with this."

Claire felt a wave of relief. They were close. Closer than they had been all night. "Thank you, Ethan," she said again.

He nodded, turning onto a quieter street. "Just hang tight. We'll be there in a minute."

But as they turned a corner, Claire's heart sank. Parked along the side of the road was a black SUV, its engine running, headlights off. Two men stood outside, talking quietly, their faces partially obscured by the shadows.

"Ethan," Claire whispered, panic creeping into her voice. "Look."

Ethan's eyes flicked to the SUV. "Damn it," he muttered. "They must have guessed where we were headed."

He kept driving, trying not to draw attention, but the men turned and spotted them immediately. One of them reached for a phone while the other started moving toward their car.

"They know it's us," Maggie said, fear in her voice.

Ethan swore under his breath. "Hang on. We're not stopping."

He hit the gas, the car lurching forward. The men shouted, one of them running back toward the SUV, but Ethan sped past them, taking a sharp turn down another side street. The SUV's engine roared to life behind them.

"Do they have a way to track us?" Claire asked her voice tight with fear.

"Probably," Ethan replied, gripping the wheel. "But we're almost there. We just need to lose them for a few minutes."

The chase was on again. The SUV sped after them, its headlights glaring in the rearview mirror. Ethan weaved through the narrow streets, taking sharp turns and speeding through intersections, trying to put distance between them and their pursuers.

Claire's heart pounded in her chest; her hands clenched into fists. She glanced at Maggie, who looked terrified but determined, and then back at Ethan. "Can you lose them?"

Ethan nodded, his eyes focused on the road. "I know a place, a parking garage up ahead. We can hide there and buy some time."

He turned sharply, the car skidding slightly as they sped toward the entrance of a multi-level parking garage. The SUV was right behind them, closing the gap.

"Hold on," Ethan muttered, steering them up the ramp and into the maze of concrete levels. He took a sharp turn up to the second level, then another, driving them deeper into the structure.

The SUV followed, its headlights flashing in the mirrors. Ethan took another turn, then abruptly cut the engine and the lights. They sat in silence, hidden in the shadows.

"Stay quiet," Ethan whispered. "Maybe they'll think we went up another level."

Claire held her breath, listening. The SUV roared past, its engine echoing through the garage, then took a turn up the ramp to the next level. Claire exhaled slowly, her heart still racing.

"They're gone," Maggie whispered. "At least for now."

Ethan nodded, his voice low. "We don't have much time. As soon as they're out of sight, we make a run for Sarah's office."

Claire nodded. "We need to move quickly. This is our only chance."

They waited for a few more tense minutes, then Ethan restarted the engine and slowly drove down the ramp, keeping to the shadows. As they exited the garage, they saw the SUV on the upper level, its headlights searching.

"We're clear," Ethan said, relief in his voice. "Let's get to Sarah before they figure it out."

They sped toward the city center, weaving through the quiet streets. Sarah's office was only a few blocks away. Claire could feel her heart racing, a mix of fear and hope. They were so close.

"There it is," Ethan said, pointing to a small building ahead with a lit sign: *Wilmington Gazette*.

Claire felt a wave of relief wash over her as she saw the sign for the *Wilmington Gazette*. The building was small, with a modest facade that looked almost nondescript in the quiet street. But inside was their chance, maybe their only chance, to expose the truth.

Ethan parked the car in a narrow alley beside the building, keeping it out of sight from the main road. He turned to Claire and Maggie, his voice low and urgent. "We need to move quickly. They'll realize we've doubled back soon enough."

Claire nodded, clutching the journal tightly against her chest. "Let's go."

They climbed out of the car and made their way to the front door. Ethan knocked a sharp, urgent rap that echoed in the stillness of the night. A moment later, the door opened a crack, and a woman with short, dark hair and piercing eyes peered out.

"Ethan?" she whispered, glancing behind them. "What's going on?"

"Sarah," Ethan replied, "It's them, the ones I told you about. We have proof. We need to get inside now."

Sarah's eyes widened slightly, but she didn't hesitate. She opened the door wider and motioned them inside. "Come on, hurry."

They slipped into the building, and Sarah quickly shut the door behind them, locking it and pulling down the shades. "Okay," she said, turning to face them, "tell me what you've got."

Ethan nodded to Claire, who stepped forward and handed Sarah the journal. "This belonged to my mother," she explained, her voice steady but urgent. "She was investigating a secret group in Topsail that's been hiding things for generations. She found something they wanted to keep buried... and they killed her for it."

Sarah took the journal, her brow furrowing as she flipped through the pages. "And are these men the same ones who've been after you?"

Claire nodded. "Yes, they've been chasing us since we found this. They won't stop until they get it back... or until we're dead."

Sarah's face grew serious as she read further. "This is... big," she murmured, almost to herself. "If half of what's in here is true, this could expose a lot of powerful people."

Ethan nodded. "That's why we need your help, Sarah. You have the contacts and the reach to get this story out there. We need to shine a light on this before they have a chance to bury it again."

Sarah's eyes narrowed with determination. "Alright. But we need to act fast. They'll come looking for you here, especially if they know you're trying to go public."

"What do we do?" Maggie asked, glancing nervously toward the windows.

Sarah motioned for them to follow her. "I have a secure room in the back where we can lay low while I make some calls. I'll reach out to some of my trusted contacts. We'll need to get this to a national outlet, somewhere they can't reach."

Claire and Maggie exchanged a look, then nodded. "Okay," Claire said. "We trust you."

They followed Sarah down a narrow hallway to a small, windowless room at the back of the building. Inside, there was a desk cluttered with papers, a few chairs, and a computer monitor glowing softly in the dim light. Sarah closed the door behind them, then moved to her desk and began dialing a number on her phone.

"Stay here," she whispered. "Keep quiet. I'll be right outside. And don't open the door unless it's me."

Ethan nodded, moving to stand by the door and listen intently. Claire and Maggie sat down, their nerves taut, their eyes on Sarah as she spoke in hushed tones into the phone.

Claire tried to calm her racing heart. They had made it this far, but they weren't safe yet. "What do you think?" she whispered to Ethan.

Ethan kept his eyes on the door, his voice low. "I think Sarah's our best shot. She knows people who can get this story out. If we can get the proof into the right hands, they won't be able to cover it up this time."

Maggie nodded, though she still looked uneasy. "I hope you're right," she murmured.

Minutes passed, each one feeling like an eternity. Claire strained to hear any sound from outside, any hint that their pursuers had found them. But all was quiet, save for the faint murmur of Sarah's voice.

Finally, Sarah returned, her expression grave but resolute. "I've reached out to a few people I trust," she said. "We're going to get this out to a couple of major networks. They're interested in the story, but they need more names, documents, and evidence. We'll have to be ready to move fast."

Ethan nodded. "What's the plan?"

Sarah glanced at Claire. "You said your mother was working with someone else, someone local, who might have more information?"

Claire thought back to the entries in her mother's journal. "Yes, there was someone... a woman named *Nancy Collins*. She runs a small bookstore on Topsail Beach. My mom mentioned meeting her several times."

Sarah's eyes brightened with recognition. "I know Nancy. She's always had a reputation for knowing the town's secrets. If she's involved, she might have more information, maybe even documents or records that could corroborate what's in the journal."

"We should go to her," Claire said. "If she knows something, she could help us make sense of all this."

Sarah hesitated. "It's a risk. Going back... they'll be watching the town, especially after tonight."

Ethan nodded. "But it's a risk we have to take. If Nancy has more proof, it could be the nail in the coffin for these guys."

Sarah considered for a moment, then nodded. "Alright. I'll go with you. We'll take my car, which is less conspicuous. But we need to be fast and careful. Once we have everything, we head straight back here, and I'll get it out to my contacts."

Claire felt a surge of determination. "Let's do it."

They moved quickly, leaving the secure room and making their way back to the front of the building. The street outside was still quiet, but there was tension in the air as if the darkness itself was holding its breath.

Sarah led them to her car, a small, nondescript sedan parked in a narrow alley. They climbed in, Ethan taking the front passenger seat and Claire and Maggie in the back. Sarah started the engine, pulling out slowly onto the street, her eyes scanning for any sign of their pursuers.

"Stay low," she murmured, "and keep an eye out."

They drove through the city in silence, the tension in the car thick. Claire kept her eyes on the rearview mirror, half-expecting to see the SUV's headlights at any moment. But the streets remained empty, and they soon reached the highway leading back toward Topsail.

As they drove, Claire's mind raced. She thought of her mother, of everything she had risked to uncover the truth and the secrets that had cost her her life. She felt a swell of determination; she would not let her mother's sacrifice be in vain.

They reached Surf City and turned down the main road. The small town was quiet, the shops and houses dark, the streets empty. Sarah drove carefully, avoiding the main streets as much as possible, taking a back road that led to the small bookstore.

They pulled outside *Quarter Moon Books*, a quaint shop with a wooden sign. The windows were dark, but there was a light on in the back. Claire felt a flicker of hope Nancy was still there.

"Let's go," Sarah whispered. "But keep your eyes open. We don't know who might be watching."

They got out of the car and approached the shop quietly. Claire knocked on the door, a soft but insistent tap. After a moment, the door opened a crack, and Nancy's face appeared, her eyes wide with surprise.

"Claire?" she whispered, glancing around nervously. "What are you doing here? It's not safe."

"I know," Claire replied. "But we need your help. My mother... she told me you might know more about what's going on. About the group."

Nancy's face paled slightly, but she nodded and quickly ushered them inside, glancing up and down the street before shutting and locking the door behind them. The interior of *Quarter Moon Books* was dimly lit, the warm glow of a single lamp casting long shadows over the packed bookshelves. The scent of old paper and coffee filled the air, comforting but heavy with secrets.

Nancy turned to face them, her expression a mix of concern and urgency. "I thought you might come," she said, her voice barely above a whisper. "After your mother... after what happened, I knew it wouldn't be long before they tried to silence anyone who knew too much."

Claire nodded, stepping closer. "My mother was trying to find the truth, and now we're trying to finish what she started. We found her journal with names and dates, but we need more. We need proof that can't be denied."

Nancy's face grew serious, and she glanced toward the back of the shop, where a heavy curtain separated the main room from a small office. "Come with me," she said, her voice still hushed. "There are things I've kept hidden, things I never wanted to see the light of day... but I think now is the time."

She led them through the curtain into the back room, a cramped space filled with stacks of papers, old ledgers, and faded photographs. A small desk sat against the far wall, cluttered with loose sheets and dusty books. Nancy moved quickly, pulling open a drawer and retrieving a thick envelope.

"These," she said, handing the envelope to Claire. "These are copies of records I managed to collect over the years. Newspaper clippings, old council meeting notes, letters, everything I could find that connects this group to what's been happening in this town."

Claire took the envelope, her hands trembling slightly as she opened it and began to sift through the contents. Her eyes widened as she saw the scope of what Nancy had gathered: documents detailing missing person cases, property records that linked prominent town members to a series of mysterious land deals, and letters that hinted at something much darker, a pact made generations ago, that seemed to bind certain families to secrecy.

Maggie peered over her shoulder, her eyes growing wide. "This is... this is huge," she whispered. "If we can get this to the press..."

Nancy nodded gravely. "But you have to be careful. This group... they have eyes everywhere. They've been keeping the secrets of Topsail for over a century. They won't hesitate to do whatever it takes to keep it hidden."

Ethan, who had been standing by the door, moved closer, his face grim. "We need to get these back to Wilmington, to Sarah's office. We'll scan them, make digital copies, and send them to every contact we have. The more people who see this, the harder it will be for them to cover it up."

Nancy looked worried. "Getting back to Wilmington won't be easy. If they're onto you, they'll be watching every road."

Sarah nodded in agreement. "We'll have to be smart about this. Is there another way out of town, something less obvious?"

Nancy hesitated, then nodded. "There's an old service road that runs parallel to the main highway. It's not on any map—it was used by fishermen back in the day. It's rough, but it leads to the old ferry docks. From there, you could cross and avoid the main routes."

Ethan's eyes brightened. "That could work. If we can get to those docks and find a way across, we'll have a head start."

Claire nodded, determination filling her. "Let's do it. We don't have time to waste."

Nancy grabbed a small flashlight from her desk and handed it to Claire. "Take this, and be careful. I'll stay here and try to cover for you if anyone comes asking."

"Thank you, Nancy," Claire said, her voice filled with gratitude. "You've done more than enough."

Nancy gave her a sad smile. "Your mother was a good woman, Claire. She deserved better than what happened to her. Be safe, and make sure the truth comes out."

With that, they slipped back through the curtain and moved toward the front door. Sarah peeked through the window, making sure the street was still clear. "Alright," she whispered. "Let's go."

They moved quickly, stepping out into the cool night air. The town was quiet; the only sound was the faint wind rustling through the trees. Sarah led them down a narrow alley that ran behind the row of shops, heading toward the outskirts of town.

As they neared the end of the alley, Claire caught sight of movement in the shadows—a figure darting quickly between two buildings. Her heart jumped, and she grabbed Sarah's arm. "Wait," she whispered. "Someone's there."

Ethan turned, his hand instinctively moving to his side. "Did they see us?"

Claire shook her head, squinting into the darkness. "I don't know… but we need to be careful."

They waited, pressed against the side of a building, listening for any sound. The seconds stretched on, and Claire's breath felt shallow in her chest. Then, suddenly, they heard it—the faint crunch of footsteps on gravel, getting closer.

Sarah motioned for them to move, and they continued down the alley, keeping low and sticking to the shadows. They reached the end and slipped out onto a narrow side street, staying close to the buildings.

The footsteps grew louder and more hurried. Claire glanced back and saw a figure emerging from the alley, moving quickly. The man's face was partially hidden by a hat, but his posture was tense and focused.

"Keep moving," Sarah urged. "We're almost there."

They picked up the pace, rounding a corner onto a dirt road leading toward the edge of town. In the distance, Claire could see the outline of an old wooden fence and, beyond that, a narrow path that seemed to disappear into the trees.

"That's it," Nancy had said. "The service road."

They reached the path and ducked into the undergrowth, moving quickly down the narrow trail. The sounds of pursuit grew fainter, but Claire's heart was still racing. She could feel the urgency of the moment, the weight of what they were carrying, what they were trying to do.

The path wound through the woods, branches reaching out like skeletal arms in the dark. They moved carefully, using the flashlight sparingly, keeping their steps quiet. After what felt like hours but was only minutes, they emerged onto a rough, gravel road. Ahead, they could see the faint glimmer of moonlight reflecting off the water.

"The docks are just ahead," Ethan whispered. "We need to find a boat, something we can use to get across the water."

They hurried forward, and soon, the old docks came into view—a collection of weathered wooden platforms jutting out over the water. A few small boats were tied up, their outlines barely visible in the dark.

"We'll take one of those," Sarah said, pointing to a small motorboat. "If it has fuel, we can get across quickly."

They approached the boat cautiously, Ethan checking the fuel tank and nodding. "There's enough to get us across, but we'll have to move fast."

Claire climbed in, helping Maggie and Sarah, while Ethan untied the rope and started the engine. The motor sputtered, then roared to life, and they pulled away from the dock, heading out into the dark water.

Behind them, Claire heard a shout—a man's voice, sharp and angry. She turned and saw a flashlight beam sweeping across the trees. Their pursuers had found the service road.

"They're coming!" she yelled.

Ethan pushed the throttle forward, and the boat surged ahead, cutting through the water's surface. The strong current pulled them slightly off course, but Ethan kept them steady, guiding the boat toward the opposite shore.

The shouts grew louder, and Claire saw the flash of headlights near the docks. The men had arrived, and she could hear the sounds of a car door slamming and feet pounding on wood.

"They have a boat too!" Maggie cried, pointing to the docks where another boat was being untied.

"Just keep going!" Ethan shouted, his voice tense.

The channel was wide, and the opposite shore was still a distant silhouette. Claire felt the wind whip at her face, the cold spray of water stinging her skin. The boat behind them was gaining speed, its engine louder now, the sound cutting through the night air.

"We're not going to make it before they catch up," Sarah said, her voice tight with fear.

Claire's mind raced. She thought of her mother, of everything she had uncovered, the secrets she had died for. She glanced at Ethan, then at Sarah. "We have to split up," she said suddenly.

"What?" Ethan shouted over the wind.

"Take the journal," Claire insisted, thrusting it into Sarah's hands. "Get to Wilmington. I'll slow them down. They're after me, not you."

"No!" Maggie protested. "You can't!"

But Claire was already moving, grabbing the flashlight and a rope. "I'll jump in the water and swim for it. They'll follow me. You keep going!"

Ethan looked torn, but he nodded. "Alright, but be careful, Claire."

Claire nodded, her heart pounding. She moved to the side of the boat, her eyes on the approaching shore. "Now!" she shouted.

She leaped into the cold water, disappearing into the dark as the boat sped ahead, carrying the truth toward safety.

Chapter 11:
The Divergence

The cold water swallowed Claire in an instant, the shock of it stealing her breath and numbing her limbs. She fought the instinct to gasp, forcing herself to stay calm as the current pulled her under. She kicked hard, propelling herself upward, her head breaking the surface with a gulp of air. The water was choppy, the current strong, and she struggled to keep her head above the waves.

She glanced back toward the boats. Ethan's boat was speeding ahead, cutting through the water toward the opposite shore. Behind it, the pursuing boat had slowed, its driver confused by her sudden disappearance. Claire saw the beam of a flashlight sweep across the water, the men searching for her. She took a deep breath and dove beneath the surface again, her heart racing.

She swam hard, staying low, the cold water biting at her skin. She knew she needed to put distance between herself and the boats, to draw the men away so that Ethan, Sarah, and Maggie could reach Wilmington safely. The current was stronger than she expected, pulling her sideways, but she fought against it, pushing herself forward.

When she surfaced again, she was farther downstream, the sounds of the boats now distant. She could hear the faint shouts of the men, their voices muffled by the wind and water. She turned, scanning the shoreline. She needed to find a place to hide, somewhere they wouldn't think to look.

The shore was closer now, and she could make out the silhouette of a large rock jutting out over the water. She swam toward it, her muscles aching with the effort. When she reached the rock, she grabbed hold of the edge, pulling herself up and clambering onto the slippery surface. She lay flat, trying to catch her breath, her eyes fixed on the boats.

The men were still searching, their flashlights scanning the water. Claire knew it wouldn't be long before they realized she wasn't in the water anymore. She needed to move, to find better cover before they decided to search the banks.

She slipped off the rock, staying low, and crawled along the bank's edge, using the thick reeds and tall grasses as cover. Her clothes were soaked, clinging to her skin, and she could feel the cold seeping into her bones, but she forced herself to keep going.

After a few minutes, she reached a small inlet where the water curved sharply. The bank here was steeper, with a cluster of trees and thick underbrush providing some shelter. She crouched down behind a large bush, shivering, and listened.

The sounds of the boats were growing louder again. Claire's heart pounded in her chest as she saw the beam of a flashlight sweeping along the bank, getting closer. She pressed herself deeper into the undergrowth, barely daring to breathe. The men were searching the shoreline now, moving methodically, their flashlights darting back and forth.

"Spread out!" one of them shouted, his voice carrying over the water. "She can't have gone far!"

Claire's breath hitched in her throat. She felt a surge of panic, but she pushed it down, forcing herself to stay calm. She had to keep them distracted, to buy more time for Ethan and the others to get away.

Slowly, she reached into her pocket and pulled out the flashlight she had grabbed from the boat. She turned it on and pointed it toward the far end of the shore, then quickly switched it off again. She hoped the brief flash would catch their attention and make them think she was heading in the opposite direction.

It worked. The men shouted to each other, and she saw the beams of their flashlights turn toward the spot where she had aimed. They started moving that way, their footsteps crunching on the gravel and mud.

Claire took the opportunity and slipped deeper into the woods, moving quickly but quietly. Her shoes squelched in the mud, and the branches snagged at her clothes, but she kept going, driven by the need to stay ahead of them.

She glanced back once to see the men reaching the spot she had illuminated, confusion on their faces. She felt a small spark of satisfaction. She had bought herself a little more time, but not much. She needed a plan.

Up ahead, she saw a narrow path winding through the trees. It was faint, almost invisible in the darkness, but it seemed to lead away from the river and into the thicker part of the woods. Claire turned onto the path, hoping it might offer more cover.

The forest was dense here, the trees pressing in from all sides, their branches intertwining overhead like a canopy. The wind rustled through the leaves, and she could hear the faint calls of night birds and the distant croak of frogs. Her breath came in sharp, shallow gasps, her lungs burning with the cold.

She pressed on, her eyes scanning the shadows for any sign of movement. She knew the men wouldn't give up easily; they were determined and relentless. She needed to find a place to hide, to wait them out until they gave up or were forced to turn back.

After what felt like hours but was only minutes, Claire came upon an old, abandoned shed, half-hidden by the thick foliage. Its wooden walls were weathered and covered in moss, and the door hung slightly ajar. She hesitated for a moment, listening carefully. The woods were quiet, and the sounds of the men were growing fainter.

She pushed the door open slowly, wincing at the creak of the rusty hinges, and slipped inside. The interior was dark and musty, filled with the smell of damp wood and decay. A few old crates and broken tools were scattered on the dirt floor, and the roof sagged in the middle, a beam of moonlight piercing through a crack.

Claire moved to the back of the shed, crouching down behind a stack of crates, and tried to calm her breathing. Her clothes were soaked through, and she could feel herself shivering, her teeth chattering in the cold. But she forced herself to stay focused, to stay quiet.

Minutes passed, each one stretching out like an eternity. She could hear the men's voices again, closer this time. They were moving through the woods, their footsteps crunching on the fallen leaves and twigs.

"Check the shed!" one of them shouted. "She might be hiding in there!"

Claire's heart leaped into her throat. She felt a surge of fear but quickly pushed it down. She had to think fast. She looked around, searching for anything she could use to defend herself or create a distraction.

Her eyes landed on an old metal bucket sitting near the door. She reached for it, careful not to make any noise, and picked it up. She waited, listening as the footsteps grew louder, approaching the shed.

Just as one of the men reached the doorway, she threw the bucket as hard as she could against the far wall. The loud clang echoed through the small space, and the man jerked back, startled.

"She's in here!" he yelled, stepping back from the door.

Claire used the moment of confusion to dart out the side of the shed, slipping around the corner and into the shadows. She kept low, moving quickly through the underbrush, her heart racing.

The men were shouting now, scrambling around the shed, trying to find her. She kept moving, her steps light, using the cover of darkness and the dense foliage to her advantage. She knew she had to get back to the water to put more distance between herself and her pursuers.

She reached the edge of the woods and saw the water ahead, dark and cold under the moonlight. She could still see the faint outline of the opposite shore, a distant silhouette.

Taking a deep breath, she sprinted toward the bank, the sound of the men still close behind her. She reached the water's edge and plunged in again, the cold biting into her skin, her breath coming in sharp gasps.

She swam hard, aiming for the far shore. She could hear the shouts behind her, the men realizing she had doubled back. They were close, but she pushed herself harder, her muscles burning with effort.

Finally, she reached the opposite bank, pulling herself up onto the mud and collapsing on the ground, panting. She glanced back and saw the flashlights on the far side of the river, still searching.

She had made it... for now.

Claire lay there for a moment, catching her breath. She knew she couldn't stay here; she had to keep moving. She pushed herself up, her body aching, and began to move deeper into the woods, away from the river.

As she moved, she felt a surge of determination. Ethan, Sarah, and Maggie were on their way to Wilmington with the journal. She had done what she needed to do—give them time to escape.

Now, she just had to survive until they could bring the truth to light.

Chapter 12
The Resolution

The cold night air seemed to press in from all sides as Claire moved deeper into the woods, her body aching with fatigue and the cold clinging to her skin like a second layer. She knew she couldn't afford to stop; every moment she stayed in one place was a moment closer to being caught. The men were still searching on the opposite bank, their flashlights dancing along the shoreline, but she knew it wouldn't be long before they spread out, continuing their relentless hunt.

She kept to the thickest part of the forest, her steps careful and deliberate, listening for any sound that might give her away. Her breath came in short, sharp bursts, her muscles burning from the effort. The dense canopy above blocked out most of the moonlight, casting deep shadows across the ground, and she had to rely on her instincts and the faint outlines of the trees to guide her.

After a few minutes, she paused to catch her breath, leaning against a thick tree. She could hear the faint rustling of leaves and the distant murmur of the water behind her. She knew she was still too close. She needed to put more distance between herself and the men.

But as she stood there, she felt something else—something deeper than fear or exhaustion. It was a sense of purpose, a determination that went beyond her survival. She thought of her mother, of everything she had sacrificed to uncover the truth, to protect her daughter. Claire felt a surge of anger mixed with resolve. She wouldn't let those men get away with what they had done. She wouldn't let them bury the secrets of Topsail any longer.

She straightened, took a deep breath, and continued moving. She needed to find a place to rest and wait out the night. If she could just make it until morning, she might have a chance.

She stumbled across a narrow path that wound through the trees, barely visible in the dark. It was overgrown, covered in leaves and underbrush, but it seemed to lead away from the water and deeper into the woods. Claire decided to follow it, hoping it might offer some kind of shelter or, at the very least, a way to stay hidden.

The path twisted and turned, winding through dense thickets and patches of tall grass. Claire could feel the sting of brambles scratching at her arms and legs, but she pushed forward, ignoring the discomfort. The forest around her was eerily silent, save for the occasional rustle of leaves or the distant call of a night bird. She felt a chill run down her spine but kept moving, forcing herself to stay focused.

After what felt like an hour but could have been much less, she saw a shape ahead—a dark outline against the faint light filtering through the trees. As she got closer, she realized it was an old, abandoned cabin, partially hidden by overgrown ivy and fallen branches. The roof sagged, and the wooden walls were weathered and cracked, but it was shelter—a place to hide.

Claire approached cautiously, listening for any sound that might indicate someone else was nearby. The forest was quiet, and she felt a small flicker of hope. Maybe, just maybe, she could rest here until morning, gather her strength, and figure out her next move.

She pushed open the door, wincing at the loud creak, and stepped inside. The cabin was small and dark, with a single room cluttered with old furniture—an overturned chair, a broken table, and a rusted wood stove in the corner. She moved quickly, checking the corners and peering out the small, broken windows to make sure no one had followed her.

Satisfied that she was alone, she collapsed onto the floor, leaning against the wall. Her whole body ached, and she could feel the exhaustion weighing her down, her eyelids heavy. She knew she couldn't sleep, not yet, but she needed to rest, to think.

She closed her eyes for a moment, taking deep, steadying breaths. She thought of Ethan, Sarah, and Maggie, of the journal and the documents they were carrying. She hoped they had made it to safety, that they were already on their way to exposing the truth. She felt a wave of gratitude toward them—toward Sarah for believing them, toward Ethan for helping them, and toward Maggie for staying by her side through all of this.

Then, she heard a faint noise outside the cabin—a twig snapping, the crunch of leaves underfoot. Her eyes snapped open, and she felt her heart start to race. She listened intently, holding her breath. The noise came again, closer this time.

Someone was out there.

Claire moved quietly to the window, peering out into the darkness. At first, she saw nothing—just the shadows of the trees swaying in the wind. But then, she caught a glimpse of movement—a figure, moving carefully through the underbrush, heading toward the cabin.

She felt a surge of fear, but she quickly pushed it down. She had to stay calm, had to think. She glanced around the cabin, looking for anything she could use to defend herself. Her eyes landed on a heavy, rusted metal pipe leaning against the wall. She grabbed it, gripping it tightly in her hands, and moved back to the door, pressing herself against the wall beside it.

The footsteps grew louder and closer. She could hear the faint rustle of clothing and the steady rhythm of someone breathing. Whoever it was, they were moving slowly, cautiously.

Claire tightened her grip on the pipe, her muscles tensed, ready to swing. She waited, her breath shallow, her heart pounding in her chest.

The footsteps stopped right outside the door. Claire held her breath, her senses on high alert. She could hear her own heartbeat and could feel the adrenaline coursing through her veins.

Then, the door creaked open slowly as if someone outside was checking to see if anyone was inside.

Claire waited, her body coiled like a spring. She saw a hand on the edge of the door, then the faint outline of a face peeking through the crack. She didn't wait any longer. With a burst of energy, she swung the pipe toward the door, aiming for the figure.

"Wait!" a voice shouted just before the pipe connected with the doorframe.

Claire froze mid-swing, the voice familiar. She hesitated, her heart racing, and the figure stepped inside, hands raised in surrender.

"Claire! It's me!" The voice came again, and Claire's eyes widened in recognition.

"Ethan?" she whispered, lowering the pipe, confusion, and relief flooding over her.

Ethan stepped fully into the cabin, lowering his hands. "Yes, it's me," he said, catching his breath. "I circled back. I had to make sure you were okay."

Claire's relief was palpable. "What are you doing here?" she asked, her voice trembling slightly. "I thought you were getting Sarah and Maggie to safety."

Ethan nodded, stepping closer. "I did. They're on their way to Wilmington to meet with Sarah's contacts. They're safe for now. But I knew you'd be in danger, trying to lead them away."

Claire shook her head, trying to steady her nerves. "I had to. It was the only way to give you time."

Ethan smiled, admiration in his eyes. "I know. And you did well. But I couldn't just leave you behind. We're in this together, remember?"

Claire felt a wave of gratitude. She had been so sure she was alone, but Ethan had come back for her. "Thank you," she whispered. "I didn't know what I was going to do next."

Ethan nodded, his expression serious. "We need to get out of here before they pick up our trail again. I know a place where we can lay low until morning, then head to Wilmington ourselves. We can meet with Sarah and Maggie there once it's safe."

Claire nodded. "Okay. Let's go."

They slipped out of the cabin, moving quietly back into the woods. Ethan led the way, his steps sure and confident. Claire followed, her heart still racing but now filled with hope. They still had a chance, a fight to win.

As they moved through the trees, she thought again of her mother and the sacrifices she had made, and she felt a surge of determination. They were close now—so close to bringing the truth to light.

And she would not stop until it was done.

Chapter 13
The Revelation

Ethan led Claire through the dense woods, his movements purposeful and quick, his eyes constantly scanning their surroundings. The cold night air seemed to press in from all sides, and the trees towered over them like silent sentinels, their branches swaying in the wind. Claire followed closely, her breath coming in short, sharp bursts, her mind racing with everything that had happened.

They moved swiftly, avoiding the main paths and sticking to the shadows. Ethan seemed to know exactly where he was going, and Claire was grateful for his confidence. She had no idea where they were, but she trusted him. He had come back for her when he didn't have to, and that meant something.

After about fifteen minutes, Ethan slowed, raising a hand to signal for Claire to stop. "We're almost there," he whispered. "There's an old fishing cabin just up ahead. It's been abandoned for years, but it should give us some cover for the night."

Claire nodded, her senses on high alert. She could feel the tension in the air, the urgency in Ethan's movements. "Do you think they're still following us?" she asked quietly.

Ethan glanced back at her, his expression serious. "Maybe, but I've thrown them off our trail for now. We just need to stay hidden until morning. Then we can figure out our next move."

They continued, moving carefully through the undergrowth. The forest was thick here, the ground uneven and covered in fallen leaves. Claire's feet ached, and her clothes were still damp from the water, but she pushed on, determined to stay strong.

Finally, they reached a small clearing, and Claire saw the cabin. It was a simple wooden structure, weathered and worn. Its roof was partially collapsed on one side. The windows were dark, and the door hung slightly open, creaking in the wind.

Ethan motioned for her to stay back, then approached the cabin cautiously, peering inside. After a moment, he turned back to Claire and nodded. "It's clear. Come on."

Claire stepped inside, immediately hit by the smell of damp wood and mildew. The cabin was bare, with only a few broken pieces of furniture scattered about and a small wood-burning stove in the corner. It wasn't much, but it would provide them with a place to rest, to regroup.

Ethan shut the door behind them and leaned against the wall, his breath heavy. "We should be safe here for a few hours," he said. "At least until the sun comes up."

Claire nodded, feeling a wave of exhaustion wash over her. She sank onto an old crate, rubbing her arms to keep warm. "I don't understand," she said after a moment, her voice filled with frustration. "How did this all start? Why would they go to such lengths to keep these secrets buried?"

Ethan sighed, crossing his arms. "It's all about power and control," he replied. "This group, whoever they are, has been pulling the strings in Topsail for generations. They've kept themselves hidden in plain sight, using fear and intimidation to maintain their grip on the town. And your mother... she found something that threatened to expose them."

Claire felt a knot form in her stomach. "But what exactly did she find?" she asked. "I've been reading through her journal, and I still don't understand... why all this secrecy?"

Ethan looked thoughtful, then pulled out a small notebook from his pocket. "Before I came to meet you and Maggie, I did some digging of my own," he said, flipping through the pages. "I found records that go back decades—documents, old newspaper clippings, town council minutes. There are references to land deals, missing persons, and cover-ups... all tied to a few powerful families in the area. The same families your mother was investigating."

Claire's eyes widened. "So it's not just about Margaret Blackwell and the old curse?"

Ethan shook his head. "No, it's much more than that. It goes deeper—Margaret Blackwell may have been the starting point, but they've used her story, her legend, to hide what they're really doing. They've created a myth to cover up their crimes. And anyone who gets too close... ends up like your mother."

Claire felt a chill run down her spine. "So what are they hiding?" she whispered. "What is it they're so desperate to keep secret?"

Ethan paused as if choosing his words carefully. "I think your mother found evidence of something that goes beyond just corruption. Something... darker. I've heard rumors over the years—stories about experiments, strange rituals, people disappearing... but nothing concrete. I think they've been doing something in the marshlands, something they don't want anyone to know about."

Claire's mind raced as she tried to piece everything together. "The marshlands..." she muttered, remembering her mother's notes. "She mentioned a hidden place there... a bunker or a lab. She thought it might be connected to Margaret Blackwell."

Ethan nodded. "Exactly. And I think she was right. I found a reference to a property deed in the town records, a piece of land in the marshlands that's been kept off the books. It's been owned by the same family for generations, but there's no record of anyone living there. It's like they're trying to erase its existence."

Claire felt a surge of determination. "Then that's where we need to go," she said firmly. "We need to find this place, whatever it is, and get the proof we need."

Ethan hesitated. "It's risky, Claire. We don't know what we're walking into. And if they catch us—"

"I know," Claire interrupted, her voice steady. "But it's the only way. We can't let them keep getting away with this. My mother died trying to uncover the truth, and I won't stop until I finish what she started."

Ethan nodded slowly, a look of respect in his eyes. "Alright," he said quietly. "We'll go. But we need to be smart about this. We'll rest here for a few hours, wait for first light, then head for the marshlands. If we're lucky, we can find this place and get the evidence we need before they realize what we're doing."

Claire agreed, though her mind was still racing. She knew it was a long shot, but it was their best chance. She leaned against the wall, trying to calm her thoughts and steady her breathing. She had to stay focused and intense.

Ethan moved to the window, keeping watch. "Try to rest," he said softly. "I'll keep an eye out."

Claire nodded, closing her eyes for a moment. But sleep didn't come easily. She felt a deep unease, a sense that they were on the edge of something big, something dangerous. She thought of her mother, of all the nights she must have spent like this—waiting, hoping, searching for answers.

Finally, exhaustion took over, and she drifted into a fitful sleep, her dreams filled with shadows and whispers, with the faces of those who had disappeared, their eyes pleading for justice.

Claire woke to the first light of dawn streaming through the cracked window. Ethan was still by the window, his eyes alert. He turned to her, a faint smile on his lips. "Ready?"

Claire nodded, feeling a renewed sense of determination. "Let's go," she said, standing up and stretching her sore muscles.

They left the cabin quietly, moving back through the woods toward the water. The air was crisp and cold, the ground still wet with dew. They kept to the shadows, their footsteps light and quick.

They reached the edge of the marshlands and paused. The landscape stretched out before them—a wide expanse of reeds and shallow water, mist rising from the ground in the early morning light. Claire could see the faint outline of something in the distance, half-hidden by the fog.

"There," Ethan said, pointing. "That's where the property is supposed to be. If we're going to find anything, it'll be there."

They moved carefully into the marsh, the ground soft and spongy underfoot. The water was cold, seeping through their shoes as they waded through the shallow pools. The reeds rustled around them, and Claire could hear the distant cry of a bird overhead.

They reached a small clearing, and Claire saw a low, concrete structure partially obscured by tall grass. It looked like an old bunker, its entrance covered with a rusted metal door. Her heart began to race.

"That must be it," she whispered.

Ethan nodded, moving closer. "Let's find out."

They approached the door, and Claire reached out, gripping the handle. It was cold and stiff, but it turned with a loud creak. She pushed the door open, and they peered inside.

The interior was dark and musty, a long hallway stretching out before them. Claire could see faint light filtering in from a crack in the ceiling, illuminating the dusty floor. She felt a chill run down her spine.

"Stay close," Ethan whispered. "We don't know what's in here."

They stepped inside, their footsteps echoing in the narrow corridor. The air was thick, filled with the smell of mold and decay. They moved slowly, their eyes scanning the shadows, searching for any sign of what this place had been used for.

As they reached the end of the hallway, they came to a heavy metal door, slightly ajar. Claire pushed it open, and they stepped into a larger room. The walls were lined with old cabinets and shelves filled with papers and files. In the center of the room was a large metal table covered with dust, yellowed with a wary look. The flickering light made the shadows dance along the walls, and the distant sound of dripping water echoed down the corridor. Ethan turned back to Claire, his expression tense. "Stay close," he whispered. "We're not alone."

Claire's heart pounded in her chest as she moved to his side, gripping the edge of the metal table for support. She strained her ears, listening for any sound. The air felt heavy, almost suffocating, as if the very walls were holding their breath.

Then she heard it again—a faint, metallic clink, followed by the sound of footsteps, soft but deliberate, moving closer. Claire's grip tightened on the table, and her mind raced. Someone else was in the bunker, and they were getting closer.

Ethan held up a finger to his lips, signaling for silence, and then gestured for Claire to follow him toward a narrow doorway at the back of the room. Claire nodded, moving as quietly as she could, her eyes never leaving the hallway.

They slipped through the doorway into a smaller, darker room, shutting the door softly behind them. The room was cramped, filled with dusty shelves and more boxes of old files and equipment. Claire's breath was shallow, her senses on high alert. She could feel Ethan beside her, his presence a comforting reminder that she wasn't alone.

The footsteps grew louder, now accompanied by the faint sound of whispering, as if whoever was outside was communicating with someone else. Claire's stomach tightened with fear. She couldn't make out the words, but the tone was urgent, almost frantic.

Ethan leaned in close, his voice barely audible. "We need to find another way out," he whispered. "They're searching the rooms. If they find us in here, we're trapped."

Claire nodded, glancing around the small room. Her eyes landed on a metal grate on the floor, partially hidden beneath a stack of old crates. She pointed to it, her voice a whisper. "What about that? It looks like a vent or a drain. Maybe it leads somewhere."

Ethan moved quickly, crouching down to inspect the grate. He tugged at it, and after a moment of resistance, it came loose with a loud scrape. Claire winced at the noise, but there was no time to worry about being quiet. Ethan looked down into the dark hole, his face grim.

"It's a ventilation shaft," he said. "It might lead outside or at least to another part of the bunker. But it's a tight fit."

Claire nodded. "We don't have a choice," she whispered. "We need to get out of here."

Ethan helped her down into the shaft first, the metal cool against her hands as she lowered herself into the narrow space. The air was stale and musty, and she had to crouch low to avoid hitting her head on the low ceiling. Ethan followed her, pulling the grate back into place above them as best he could.

They crawled forward, the shaft barely wide enough for them to move. The metal creaked under their weight, and every sound seemed magnified in the confined space. Claire felt the walls pressing in around her, but she forced herself to keep going, to stay calm.

After a few minutes, they reached a bend in the shaft. Ethan motioned for her to stop, then leaned forward, listening. Claire could hear it too—the sound of the footsteps growing louder, echoing through the ventilation system. The men were close.

Ethan turned to her, his expression serious. "We need to keep moving," he whispered. "They're right behind us."

Claire nodded, crawling faster, the metal scraping against her hands and knees. She could feel her heart racing, her breath coming in quick, shallow gasps. The shaft was dark, and she could barely see where she was going, but she kept moving, following the faint draft of air that suggested an exit up ahead.

The shaft opened into a small, square chamber with another grate on the far wall. Ethan moved to it, pushing against the metal bars. After a moment, the grate gave way, and he pulled it free, revealing a narrow opening that led into another hallway.

Claire hesitated. "Do you think it's safe?" she whispered.

Ethan glanced out, then nodded. "Safer than staying in here. Come on."

They climbed out of the shaft and into the hallway, pressing themselves against the wall. The corridor was dimly lit by a single flickering bulb overhead, casting long shadows on the cracked concrete floor. The air felt cooler here, fresher, and Claire realized they must be closer to the surface.

"This way," Ethan said, nodding toward a set of stairs at the end of the hallway. "We need to get to higher ground."

They moved quickly but cautiously, keeping to the shadows as they made their way down the corridor. The sound of footsteps was still audible, but it was more distant now, echoing through the maze of rooms and passageways. Claire felt a flicker of hope—maybe they had lost them.

They reached the staircase and began to climb, the steps creaking under their weight. Claire felt her muscles burning with every step, her breath coming in sharp bursts, but she pushed herself to keep going. She could see a door at the top of the stairs, a faint sliver of light leaking through the cracks.

When they reached the door, Ethan paused, listening for any sound on the other side. He glanced back at Claire, then slowly pushed the door open.

They stepped out into the cool morning air, the sunlight blinding after the darkness of the bunker. Claire blinked, her eyes adjusting to the light, and saw that they were outside, standing on a small, overgrown path that led into the thick of the marshlands. The bunker's entrance was hidden by tall reeds and undergrowth, making it nearly invisible from a distance.

Ethan shut the door softly behind them, then turned to Claire. "We need to keep moving," he said. "If they realize we're gone, they'll come looking."

Claire nodded, taking a deep breath. "Where do we go now?"

Ethan pointed to the north. "There's a road that leads out of the marsh, about a mile that way. If we can make it there, we might find a car or at least get far enough away to make contact with Sarah and Maggie."

Claire felt a surge of determination. "Okay, let's go."

They moved quickly, pushing through the tall grasses and reeds, the ground soft and uneven beneath their feet. The marsh was quiet; the only sound was the distant call of a bird overhead and the rustling of the wind through the grasses. Claire felt a sense of urgency, a need to get as far away from the bunker as possible.

As they walked, she turned to Ethan. "What do you think they were doing in there?" she asked quietly.

Ethan shook his head. "I don't know. But whatever it was, it wasn't good. Those names, those experiments... they've been hiding something for a long time. And we need to make sure the world knows about it."

They continued on, the road slowly coming into view ahead, a narrow strip of dirt cutting through the marsh. Claire felt a flicker of hope—they were almost there. If they could just reach the road, they might have a chance to escape.

But then, suddenly, she heard it—a low rumble, growing louder. Her heart sank as she realized what it was.

A car engine.

She glanced at Ethan, who nodded grimly. "They've found us," he muttered.

They hurried toward the road, but the sound of the engine was getting closer, the roar of the tires on the gravel unmistakable. Claire felt a surge of panic, but she forced herself to stay calm.

"We need to hide," she whispered, looking around frantically. "Quickly!"

Ethan nodded, pulling her toward a dense cluster of reeds near the side of the road. They crouched down, trying to make themselves as small as possible, their breath coming in quick, shallow bursts.

The car appeared over the rise—a black SUV, its headlights cutting through the morning mist. It slowed as it reached the spot where they had planned to cross, its engine idling.

Claire held her breath, her heart pounding in her chest. She could see the men inside, their faces tense and alert, scanning the area. She prayed they wouldn't see them and that they would keep driving.

But the SUV came to a full stop, and one of the men climbed out, a gun in his hand. He looked around, his eyes narrowing.

Claire's grip tightened on Ethan's arm. "What do we do?" she whispered, panic creeping into her voice.

Ethan leaned close, his voice calm and steady. "Stay still. Don't move a muscle."

The man walked toward the reeds, his steps slow and deliberate. Claire could see the gun in his hand, gleaming in the light. She felt her pulse quicken, every nerve in her body screaming at her to run, but she stayed still, willing herself to be invisible.

The man stopped just a few feet away, his eyes scanning the reeds. Claire could see the tension in his posture, the readiness to strike. She held her breath, her heart pounding so loudly she feared he would hear it.

And then, suddenly, there was a shout from the SUV. "Come on! We don't have time for this!"

The man hesitated for a moment, then turned and walked back to the car, frustration etched on his face. He climbed back in, and the SUV's engine roared to life again, the vehicle speeding down the road and out of sight.

Claire let out a shaky breath, her body trembling with relief. Ethan squeezed her arm gently. "We're okay," he whispered. "For now."

Claire nodded, her body still tense, feeling the adrenaline coursing through her veins. She forced herself to take a deep breath, calming her nerves. "We need to move before they change their minds," she whispered, her voice low but urgent.

Ethan nodded, glancing up and down the road. "Let's go, but we have to stay off the road," he replied. "We'll follow it from a distance, through the marsh. They might double back."

They kept low, moving parallel to the road but staying hidden among the tall grasses and reeds. The air smelled of salt and earth, and the morning mist clung to their skin like a damp cloak. Claire's heart pounded as they walked, her eyes scanning the road ahead for any sign of movement.

They had been walking for several minutes when Claire saw a small, abandoned shack on the other side of the road, half-hidden by a cluster of trees. It looked old and run-down, with a sagging roof and walls covered in vines, but it was shelter—a place to hide and regroup.

"Look," Claire whispered, pointing to the shack. "Maybe we can rest there for a minute and figure out our next move."

Ethan followed her gaze, then nodded. "It's worth a shot. Let's cross, but stay low."

They crouched down and quickly crossed the road, creeping. The shack was even more dilapidated up close; the door hung on a single hinge, and the windows were broken, shards of glass scattered. Ethan pushed the door open carefully, and they slipped inside.

The interior was small and cramped, with a dirt floor and a few broken pieces of furniture. A rusted metal stove sat in one corner, and an old mattress lay on the floor, covered in dust and cobwebs. Claire felt a shiver run down her spine, but it was better than being out in the open.

Ethan closed the door behind them and peered out to the window. "I don't see anyone," he said, his voice low. "But we can't stay here long. We need to keep moving."

Claire nodded, feeling the weight of exhaustion settling into her bones. "Where do we go from here?" she asked. "They're watching the roads, and we're running out of places to hide."

Ethan turned back to her, his expression serious. "We need to get back to Wilmington," he said. "Sarah and Maggie are probably waiting for us. If we can reach them, we'll have a better chance of getting this story out to the press."

"But how?" Claire asked. "We don't have a car, and the roads are being watched."

Ethan thought for a moment, then nodded to himself. "There's an old train track that runs through the marshlands," he said. "It's not used much anymore, but it leads straight into Wilmington. If we can find it, we can follow it back to the city without being seen."

Claire felt a flicker of hope. "Okay," she agreed. "Let's find it."

They slipped out of the shack and returned to the reeds' cover. The morning mist was lifting, and the sun was just starting to break through the clouds, casting long shadows across the marsh. They moved quickly, keeping their heads low, searching for any sign of the train tracks.

After several minutes of walking, they saw a narrow, overgrown path cutting through the tall grass, the rusted metal rails barely visible beneath the thick undergrowth. Claire felt a surge of relief. "There," she whispered, pointing. "That's got to be it."

Ethan nodded. "Good eyes," he said. "Let's follow it. Stay close to the edges and keep low."

They stepped onto the tracks and began to move, staying close to the tall grass on either side. The ground was uneven, and the old wooden ties creaked under their weight, but they kept moving, their pace steady.

The tracks wound through the marsh, following a narrow strip of higher ground. The air was thick with the sounds of the marsh—frogs croaking, birds calling, and the distant rustle of reeds in the wind.

Claire felt her nerves start to calm; the rhythm of their steps was almost soothing.

But as they continued, Claire noticed something in the distance—a figure moving along the tracks ahead of them. She froze, her heart leaping into her throat. "Ethan," she whispered urgently, grabbing his arm.

Ethan stopped and followed her gaze. The figure was far ahead, partially obscured by the mist, but it was moving toward them, slowly and cautiously. Claire felt a surge of fear. Were they being followed again?

Ethan narrowed his eyes. "Stay behind me," he said quietly, reaching into his pocket and pulling out a small flashlight. "Let's see who this is."

They moved closer, their steps careful and silent. As they neared, the figure became clearer—a man dressed in a long coat, his face partially hidden by a hood. He seemed to be searching for something, his head turning from side to side.

Ethan held up the flashlight, clicking it on briefly. "Hey!" he called out, his voice firm but not aggressive. "Who are you?"

The man froze, then slowly raised his hands. "Don't shoot," he called back, his voice thin and tired. "I'm not one of them."

Ethan and Claire exchanged a glance. "Come closer," Ethan said cautiously.

The man hesitated, then stepped forward into the light. As he did, Claire recognized him—*Jim*, the rideshare driver who had helped them earlier. His face was lined with worry, and a bruise formed on his cheek.

"Jim?" Claire said, surprised. "What are you doing here?"

Jim lowered his hands, his expression tense. "I was trying to find you," he said. "After I dropped you off and saw those men, I knew something wasn't right. I doubled back, but they caught up with me. Managed to get away, but I figured you might need help."

Claire felt a mix of relief and caution. "You came back for us?"

Jim nodded. "I know these guys," he said quietly. "They're not the kind you mess with. If they're after you, there's a reason, and it has to be something big. I thought... maybe I could help."

Ethan studied Jim's face, searching for any sign of deception. "And why should we trust you?" he asked.

Jim shrugged, a faint smile on his lips. "You shouldn't," he admitted. "But I've lived in this town my whole life. I know what's been happening, and I've seen too many people disappear. I want to help put a stop to it."

Claire nodded slowly. "Alright, Jim. We could use all the help we can get. Do you know how we can get to Wilmington safely?"

Jim looked relieved. "Yeah," he said. "There's an old maintenance shed a little further up the tracks. If we can get there, I've got a car stashed. It's hidden, and they won't know to look for it. We can drive the rest of the way."

Ethan glanced at Claire, then nodded. "Let's do it," he said. "Lead the way, but no tricks, Jim."

Jim nodded, turning to lead them up the tracks. They followed him carefully, watching their surroundings, every rustle and sound making them jump. The tension was thick, but they moved quickly, determined to reach safety.

After a few minutes, they saw a small maintenance shed half-hidden by overgrown bushes and trees. Jim hurried over and pulled open a hidden door on the side, revealing a narrow space where an old but sturdy-looking car was parked.

"Get in," Jim said, glancing around nervously. "I'll get us out of here."

They piled into the car, Jim in the driver's seat. He turned the key, and the engine roared to life, the sound surprisingly loud in the quiet of the marsh. Claire felt her heart race as they pulled onto a narrow dirt road, heading toward the highway.

Jim drove quickly but carefully, avoiding the main roads and sticking to the back routes. They could see the occasional flash of headlights in the distance, but no one seemed to be following them.

"Almost there," Jim said, glancing in the rearview mirror. "Just a few more minutes."

Claire felt a surge of hope. They were close—so close. They might have a chance if they could just make it to Wilmington.

And then, suddenly, a dark shape loomed ahead on the road—a truck, parked sideways, blocking their path. The headlights were off, and Claire could see the shadowy figures beside it.

Jim swore under his breath. "Damn it," he muttered, slamming on the brakes.

Ethan's eyes were wide. "They've blocked the road," he said. "They knew we'd come this way."

Jim turned to Claire, his face set with determination. "Hold on," he said. "We're not stopping."

He hit the gas, the car lurching forward toward the truck. The figures in front of them scattered, surprised by the sudden movement. Claire braced herself as the car swerved to the side, skidding off the road and into the brush.

They crashed through the undergrowth, the car bouncing over rocks and roots, but Jim kept his foot on the gas, pushing forward. The truck behind them revved its engine, trying to follow, but they were already moving away, heading toward the highway.

Claire clung to the seat, her heart pounding. "Just keep going, Jim!" she shouted, adrenaline surging through her veins. The car jolted violently as they tore through the thick brush, branches scratching against the windows like desperate hands trying to pull them back. The truck's headlights illuminated the trees, casting long, menacing shadows that seemed to chase after them.

Jim's face was tense, his knuckles white as he gripped the steering wheel. "Hold tight," he muttered. "This road's gonna get rough."

Ethan leaned forward, scanning their surroundings. "If we can make it past that bend," he said, pointing ahead to where the dirt road curved sharply, "we might lose them in the trees."

Claire glanced back. The truck was gaining, its engine roaring, but it was struggling with the uneven terrain. She turned to Ethan and nodded. "Do it, Jim. We have to lose them!"

Jim nodded, his jaw set in determination. He took the turn hard, the tires skidding on the loose gravel, and the car fishtailed before he regained control. They were moving deeper into the woods now, the trees closing in around them. The truck tried to follow, but the narrow road was slowing it down, and the headlights flickered as it maneuvered around the tight corner.

"Almost there," Jim muttered, glancing in the rearview mirror. "Just a little further."

They raced down the dirt road, the sound of the truck behind them fading. Claire could barely see in the darkness, but she felt the car begin to level out as the road straightened. Jim pushed the car faster, the engine straining with the effort.

Suddenly, the road ahead opened up into a wider path, and Claire saw a glimmer of hope—an intersection with an old paved road. If they could reach it, they could get back on a smoother surface, and maybe even lose the truck for good.

"There!" Ethan shouted. "Turn left, take us toward the city!"

Jim nodded, his face grim. "Got it!"

He turned sharply onto the paved road, the tires squealing as they hit the smoother surface. For a moment, the car felt like it was flying, speeding away from the threat behind them. Claire glanced back and saw the truck still struggling to make the turn, the headlights flickering in the distance.

"We're pulling ahead!" she said, a glimmer of relief in her voice.

Jim kept his foot on the gas, the car racing down the road. The trees were thinning out, and Claire could see the lights of Wilmington starting to appear on the horizon, faint but promising. They were so close—just a few more miles, and they'd be in the city, where they could find help, and safety, and get their story out.

But just as she began to feel hope creeping in, a loud bang echoed through the air, and the car lurched violently to the side. Claire screamed as the car skidded, the back tire blown. Jim fought to keep control, but the car was swerving dangerously.

"They shot our tire!" Ethan shouted. "Hold on!"

Jim gritted his teeth, trying to steady the car. "I can't hold it!" he yelled, his voice strained.

The car veered off the road, crashing through a wooden fence and skidding to a stop in a small field. Dust and debris filled the air as they came to a jarring halt, the front end of the car buried in the soft earth.

For a moment, everything was still, the only sound the faint ringing in Claire's ears. She gasped for breath, her heart racing, her body shaking from the impact.

"Is everyone okay?" Ethan asked, his voice urgent.

"Yeah," Claire replied, though her voice trembled. "I think so."

Jim groaned, rubbing his forehead where he had hit the steering wheel. "I'm fine," he muttered. "But the car's done for. We're on foot from here."

They scrambled out of the car, the cold night air hitting Claire's face like a slap. She could hear the truck's engine again, louder now, coming closer. "We have to move," she said, panic rising in her chest. "They'll be on us any second."

Ethan nodded, grabbing Claire's arm. "This way," he urged. "There's a creek up ahead. If we can reach it, we might be able to follow it into the city and lose them."

Jim led the way, and they sprinted across the field, their footsteps pounding against the earth. Claire's lungs burned with every breath, but she kept moving, driven by fear and adrenaline.

The truck's headlights swept across the field behind them, and she could hear the men shouting, their voices angry and determined. She glanced back and saw the truck stop at the edge of the field, the men jumping out, guns in hand.

"They're right behind us!" Maggie yelled, terror in her voice.

"Keep going!" Ethan urged, pushing them forward. "We're almost to the creek!"

They reached the edge of the field and saw a narrow stream cutting through the undergrowth, the water glinting faintly in the moonlight. Jim didn't hesitate—he jumped down into the water, and the rest followed, the cold water soaking their shoes and clothes.

"Stay low," Jim whispered, crouching in the shallow creek. "We'll follow this until we're far enough away."

They moved through the water, the creekbed slippery and uneven underfoot. The cold bit into Claire's skin, but she pushed forward, knowing they couldn't afford to stop. She could still hear the men behind them, crashing through the undergrowth, but the creek was winding, and the sounds began to fade.

After what felt like an eternity, the noise of their pursuers grew distant, and they reached a small bridge that spanned the creek. Jim stopped, his breath heavy. "We need to get out of the water," he said. "We're close to the city limits now. We should be able to find a phone, call for help."

Claire nodded, feeling her legs trembling with exhaustion. They climbed up the bank and crossed the bridge, emerging onto a narrow road. She could see the lights of Wilmington more clearly now, just a few blocks away.

"We made it," Ethan said, a mixture of relief and disbelief in his voice.

But Jim shook his head, his expression still tense. "Not yet," he replied. "We need to get to Sarah's office. If those guys are still out there, they won't give up easily. And they'll be looking for us in the city."

They hurried down the road, sticking close to the shadows. The city was waking up now, the early morning light beginning to break over the horizon. Claire felt a surge of hope—they were so close.

They turned a corner and saw the familiar sign of the *Wilmington Gazette*, the small building where they had left Sarah and Maggie. Claire felt a wave of relief wash over her. "There it is," she whispered. "We're almost there."

They ran to the door, and Jim knocked urgently. After a tense moment, the door opened, and Sarah peered out, her eyes wide with concern. "Thank God," she whispered, pulling them inside. "We were worried."

Maggie was there too, her face pale but relieved. "Are you okay?" she asked, rushing over to hug Claire. "We thought they got you."

"We're fine," Claire said, holding Maggie tightly. "But they're still out there. We have to move fast."

Sarah nodded, shutting and locking the door. "I've made contact with my sources," she said. "We have what we need. I've already sent out copies of the documents to several major networks. The story is going public today."

Claire felt a rush of gratitude and relief. "So, it's over?" she asked, almost not daring to believe it.

Sarah shook her head. "Not quite. They won't stop until they're exposed. But we have a head start. And once this goes live, they'll have nowhere to hide."

Ethan nodded, a determined look on his face. "Then let's make sure everyone knows," he said. "It's time to bring them down, once and for all."

Claire looked around the room at her friends and allies and felt a fierce determination rise within her. They had come so far and faced so much. And now, they were on the brink of finally uncovering the truth.

"We're ready," she said, her voice strong. "Let's end this."

Chapter 14
The Exposure

The tension in the room was palpable as Sarah moved quickly to her computer, her fingers flying over the keyboard. Claire, Ethan, Maggie, and Jim stood behind her, their eyes fixed on the screen. The dim light of the early morning filtered through the blinds, casting long shadows across the office. Sarah's phone buzzed with incoming messages and calls, her contacts eager to get the story she was about to break.

"Alright," Sarah muttered, her voice steady despite the adrenaline coursing through her. "I've sent everything to my sources at the major networks. They're all ready to go live. We just need to make sure we're safe until then."

Claire felt a surge of hope. "How long will it take?" she asked, glancing over at the door, half-expecting the men to burst through at any moment.

Sarah glanced at her watch. "Minutes, maybe less. I told them it was urgent. Once the story is out, we'll have to be ready for anything."

Jim moved to the window, peering through the blinds. "We should barricade the door," he suggested. "They might come here, try to stop us before it hits the news."

Ethan nodded in agreement. "Good idea. Let's stack some of those filing cabinets in front of it. Just in case."

They moved quickly, dragging heavy metal cabinets across the room and piling them against the door. The sound of metal scraping against the floor filled the air, echoing in the small space. Claire felt her pulse quicken with every movement, her nerves stretched taut.

Maggie hovered close to Claire, her eyes wide with worry. "Do you think they'll find us here?" she whispered.

Claire shook her head, though she wasn't sure. "We just have to hold out a little longer," she said, trying to sound reassuring. "Once the story breaks, they'll have to back off. They won't be able to hide anymore."

Ethan finished pushing the last cabinet into place and turned back to Sarah. "How are we doing?" he asked.

Sarah glanced at the screen, her expression tense. "It's almost there," she replied. "They're prepping for a live broadcast. Once they verify everything, it'll go out to the networks. They're already drafting articles and preparing social media posts."

Claire felt her heart pound with anticipation. She could hardly believe it was happening—the truth was finally coming to light. "What about the local police?" she asked. "Can we trust them?"

Sarah hesitated, then shook her head. "I've spoken to a few contacts, but I don't know who's in on this and who's not. Some of them might be compromised. We need to rely on the media to make sure the public knows what's going on. Once it's out, the police will have to act."

Jim remained by the window, his face tense. "Someone's coming," he said quietly, peeking through the blinds. "A car just pulled up across the street. I think it's them."

Claire's stomach dropped. "How many?"

Jim squinted, trying to get a better look. "Two men... maybe three. One of them looks like the guy who was at the roadblock."

Ethan's face darkened. "They're not going to stop until they have what they want."

Sarah nodded, still typing furiously. "Then we need to be ready. Everyone stay low. If they try to get in, we hold them off as long as we can."

They all took cover behind the desks and cabinets, waiting. The air was thick with tension, amplifying every sound in the stillness. Claire could hear the faint murmur of voices outside and the distant hum of the car engine. She gripped the edge of the desk, her knuckles white.

Then came the sound of footsteps—slow, deliberate, moving closer. The door handle rattled, and there was a soft knock, followed by a voice. "We know you're in there," the man called. "Come out, and no one gets hurt."

Claire's heart pounded in her chest. She glanced at Ethan, who shook his head. "Don't move," he whispered. "Let them make the first move."

The door rattled again, harder this time. "You can't hide forever," the voice said, more insistent now. "We just want to talk. Hand over what you have, and we'll let you go."

Sarah kept her focus on the screen, her hands steady as she typed. "Almost there," she muttered. "Come on…"

Claire held her breath, listening. The men outside were murmuring to each other, their voices low and agitated. Then, suddenly, there was a loud bang—a gunshot. The sound shattered the quiet, and Claire flinched, her heart racing.

"They're trying to scare us," Ethan said quietly. "Stay calm."

The men outside began pounding on the door, shouting angrily. The barricade held, but the noise was deafening. Claire felt a surge of fear but pushed it down. She had to stay focused and trust that the story would break before the men entered.

Sarah's phone buzzed, and she grabbed it, her eyes scanning the screen. "It's happening!" she whispered, a mix of relief and urgency in her voice. "They're going live!"

Claire felt a rush of adrenaline. "Thank God," she breathed.

Sarah clicked a few more buttons on her computer, bringing up a live stream on the screen. The image flickered for a moment, then stabilized. A news anchor appeared, looking serious, with the words **"BREAKING NEWS"** scrolling across the bottom of the screen.

"This just in," the anchor said, his tone grave. "We've received disturbing reports from Topsail, North Carolina, where a secretive group has allegedly been conducting illegal experiments and cover-ups for decades. Documents provided to us indicate that several prominent local figures may be involved in a conspiracy to hide the disappearance of multiple residents, as well as engaging in unethical medical practices."

The screen cut to an image of Margaret Blackwell, followed by photos of the documents Sarah had sent out—the property deeds, the lists of names, the experiments. Claire felt a surge of triumph. They were doing it. The world was finally seeing the truth.

The banging on the door grew louder, more frantic. One of the men outside shouted, "They're doing it! They're going live! Get in there now!"

Ethan braced himself, his eyes hard. "Get ready," he said. "They're going to try and force their way in."

Jim moved closer to the door, holding a metal pipe he'd found. "We won't make it easy for them," he muttered.

Suddenly, there was another loud bang—this time, the door shook violently as the men tried to break through. Claire's heart raced, but she felt a strange calm settle over her. They had done what they needed to do. Now, it was just a matter of holding on.

The news broadcast continued, the anchor's voice clear and strong. "These revelations have sent shockwaves through the community, and local authorities are under intense pressure to investigate. Federal agencies have already been alerted, and we expect further developments in the coming hours."

The men outside were shouting angrily now, their frustration palpable. There was another bang, and the door splintered slightly, but the barricade held firm.

Sarah turned to them, her eyes fierce. "We did it," she whispered. "The story is out. They can't stop it now."

Claire nodded, a sense of relief flooding over her. "We did it," she echoed, her voice filled with determination.

Ethan moved closer to her, his expression serious. "They're going to come in hard," he warned. "Be ready."

The door gave another loud creak, and then, suddenly, there was a shout from outside. "Get back!" one of the men yelled. "The police are coming!"

Claire felt a jolt of hope. "Did you call them?" she asked Sarah.

Sarah nodded a small smile on her lips. "I sent an alert to every contact I had. Looks like they're finally listening."

Outside, they could hear the distant wail of sirens approaching, growing louder with each passing second. The men hesitated, then scrambled back toward their car, their footsteps fading.

Moments later, the sirens were right outside the building, and Claire heard the crackle of a police radio. "This is the Wilmington Police Department! Step away from the building and put your hands up!"

The tension in the room broke all at once. Claire felt herself start to breathe again, the relief overwhelming. Maggie hugged her tightly, tears streaming down her face. "We did it," she whispered. "We're safe."

Ethan grinned, his eyes shining. "We're safe, but we're not done yet," he said. "We need to make sure these people are held accountable."

Jim chuckled, leaning against the wall. "Don't worry," he said. "With this kind of media attention, they're not going to be able to hide anymore."

Claire felt a sense of peace settles over her. They had won. They had uncovered the truth and exposed the lies, and finally, the people of Topsail would know what had been happening in their town for so many years.

The door opened, and a police officer stepped inside, his gun drawn. "Is everyone okay in here?" he asked.

Sarah nodded, her smile broad. "We're fine, officer," she said. "But I think you're going to want to hear our story."

The officer nodded, lowering his weapon. "We heard," he said. "And we're here to make sure justice is done."

Claire felt tears of relief well up in her eyes. The exhaustion, fear, and tension of the past few days seemed to drain from her all at once, replaced by an overwhelming sense of triumph. They had made it. The truth was out, and there was no going back.

The officer motioned for them to follow. "We're taking you all to the station," he said. "We need statements, and you'll be safer there until we sort this out. There's already a crowd gathering outside—reporters, too. Looks like you stirred up quite the storm."

Sarah smirked, her confidence unwavering. "Good," she replied. "The more eyes on this, the better."

They moved carefully toward the door, the police forming a protective cordon around them. Outside, the morning light was bright and blinding, and Claire blinked against it, her senses overwhelmed after so much time in the dark. She could see the flashing lights of police cars, the crowd of onlookers, and a few news vans already parked across the street.

The men who had tried to break into the office were being cuffed and led away by police officers, their faces set in expressions of anger and defeat. Claire felt a wave of satisfaction seeing them being taken away, knowing that they would no longer have the power to harm anyone.

"Come on," Ethan urged gently, guiding her forward. "We need to get out of here before things get too chaotic."

They moved toward a waiting police car, and Claire glanced back at the *Wilmington Gazette* building. It was swarming with police and reporters now, and she saw several officers speaking into radios, coordinating the scene.

As they reached the car, one of the officers spoke into his shoulder radio. "We've got them," he said. "Bringing them to the station now."

Maggie squeezed Claire's hand tightly. "It's over, Claire," she whispered, her voice filled with relief. "We did it."

Claire nodded, but a thought nagged at her. "It's not quite over yet," she said softly. "We need to make sure everyone involved is held accountable... that this isn't just swept under the rug."

Jim leaned against the car, his expression serious. "You're right," he said. "This is just the beginning. Now that the truth is out, we have to keep pushing."

Ethan nodded in agreement. "We'll keep fighting," he said firmly. "We'll make sure the authorities don't ignore this and that the victims get justice."

Claire felt a renewed sense of purpose. "Let's go, then," she said, climbing into the car. "We've got work to do."

Epilogue
The Aftermath

The next few weeks were a whirlwind. The story spread quickly, picked up by every major news outlet in the country. The people of Topsail and the nation at large were horrified by the revelations—decades of secrets, cover-ups, and the disappearance of innocent people. The pressure on local and state authorities grew, and soon, federal investigators were brought in to take over the case.

Sarah worked tirelessly, providing the media with updates and new information as it came in. Her small office became a hub of activity, with reporters and activists stopping by, eager to get involved in the fight for justice.

Claire, Ethan, and Maggie found themselves at the center of the storm, their every move watched by the public and the press. They gave interviews, spoke at rallies, and worked with the families of the victims to keep the pressure on the authorities.

The investigation uncovered more than anyone had imagined. The group responsible for the crimes was not just a small, secretive cabal but a network that reached far beyond Topsail. The names on the list Claire had found in the bunker were just the beginning. There were more victims, more secrets, and a web of corruption that spanned decades.

But for the first time in years, people were speaking out. Survivors and families of the disappeared came forward, sharing their stories, adding to the growing chorus of voices demanding justice.

The authorities, under intense scrutiny, began making arrests. Several prominent local figures, including the corrupt sheriff, were taken into custody. Dr. Victor Holcomb, who had been at the center of the experiments, was found hiding in a remote part of the state. He was arrested and charged with multiple counts, ranging from kidnapping to manslaughter. The hidden property in the marshlands was thoroughly searched, revealing more evidence of the group's illegal activities, and their operations were exposed for all to see.

For Claire, the months that followed were bittersweet. She felt a deep sense of satisfaction knowing her mother's work had not been in vain and that the secrets she had uncovered would finally see the light of day. But she also felt a profound sadness for all the lives that had been lost and for the years of pain and fear endured by so many.

One evening, Claire stood on the shore of Topsail Beach, the waves crashing softly against the sand, the sun setting in the distance. She held her mother's journal in her hands, its pages now worn and frayed from all it had been through. She turned to a page filled with her mother's neat handwriting and smiled, feeling her presence beside her.

"You did it, Mom," she whispered to the wind. "You found the truth. And we made sure everyone else did, too."

Ethan joined her, placing a comforting arm around her shoulders. "She'd be proud of you, Claire," he said softly.

Claire nodded, feeling a mix of grief and gratitude. "I know," she said. "And I'm going to keep fighting for her and for everyone who was hurt by them."

Ethan smiled. "You're not alone," he replied. "We're all in this together."

Maggie and Jim joined them, standing side by side on the shore. The four of them looked out at the ocean, the waves reflecting the colors of the sunset. They were a team now, bound together by their shared struggle and their determination to see justice done.

As the sun dipped below the horizon, Claire felt a sense of peace she hadn't known in a long time. The fight wasn't over, but they had made a start. They had brought the truth to light, and they had taken the first steps toward healing.

Together, they turned and walked back up the beach, ready to face whatever came next, knowing they had the strength to stand against the darkness.

Don't miss out!

Visit the website below and you can sign up to receive emails whenever Aaron Cross publishes a new book. There's no charge and no obligation.

https://books2read.com/r/B-A-SLWRC-XUKGF

BOOKS 2 READ

Connecting independent readers to independent writers.